STOCKHOLM SYNDROME

A Brea James
Erotic Adventure

Jaime Blaise

Stockholm syndrome is a work of fiction. All incidents and dialogue, and all characters would be exception of some well-known historical figures, are products of this author's imagination and are not to be construed as real. Where real-life historical persons appear, the situations, incidents, and dialogues concerning those persons are entirely fictional and are not intended to depict actual events or to change the entirely fictional manner of the work. In all other respects, any resemblance to persons living or dead is entirely coincidental

breajames.com

Ordering Information:
For details, contact info@breajames.com.

Print ISBN: 978-1-09839-309-0
eBook ISBN: 978-1-09839-310-6

Printed in the United States of America on SFI Certified paper.

First Edition

For Brea.

Whoever, or wherever in the world you may be.

Because you are more than you know.

But there is neither East nor West,

Border, nor Breed, nor Birth,

When two strong equals stand face to face,

Though they come from the ends of the earth.

Rudyard Kipling

1 | DHAKA

I could still feel him inside of me. The muscle memory of that delicious push of his body in mine. The thought of it was vivid and unforgettable, as was the recollection of him, this remarkable new stranger who had turned up in my life with impeccably bad timing. It had been a while, and meeting Scott ticked all the necessary requirements of abbreviated courtship; minimal effort and low expectations, while holding out the possibility for some real pleasure. Perhaps for that same reason it allowed for the kind of honest, uninhibited and absolutely more selfish satisfaction a casual, one-night stand enables. Within a few short hours after our meeting at a dry and seemingly endless industry function, our clothes were scattered across my bedroom floor and our hands were hungrily exploring each other's bodies.

Scott had interested me with his easy confidence; he possessed it with an almost unflinching sense of self-assurance I found irresistible. But it wasn't just conceit, wasn't just his male swagger that had impressed me. Even now I could easily recall the urgency of his mouth, how much he seemed to want me, how ready he was in my grasp, and most vividly of all, how he felt inside of me. It was frankly the kind of sex I needed now. Easy, uncomplicated and very, very satisfying.

"You really have to leave tomorrow?" he asked after a respectful interval.

"I'm not thrilled about it either," I replied, relishing, however temporarily, the arms around me, the smell of him on my sheets. The truth of it was that I had been looking forward to finishing up this particular assignment for a long time. I couldn't technically call it a claim, since it was about recovery and not about loss, but I was relieved that the weeks of preamble, planning and intricate negotiation would finally pay off in the next few days. Even so, the usual sense of accomplishment that came with finally tying up a deal this complicated was certainly diminished by the way my body felt right now. A feeling I would really have loved to enjoy longer. Even now, spent and sore, I wanted more of him.

"And you're going all that way just to pick up this old statue?"

"Well, there's maybe a bit more to it than that."

"Somehow I can't imagine you not getting what you want."

"I've been told I'm a pretty good negotiator," I shrugged artfully.

"Must have missed the part where we negotiated tonight," he laughed.

I rolled over to face him. "Oh, we're done negotiating," I reached down and found him pleasingly ready again. "This here is really all about sealing the deal." I motioned him above me, wanting to feel the weight of him on my body. Scott was not slow and needed no further encouragement, his kisses immediately succeeding in parting my thighs under him, easing him inside of me.

"You're smiling," he whispered.

"Imagine that," I breathed back, arching my back even further and willing him deeper as his thrusts forced me back into the pillows, drowning my moans in the sea of sheets. For that moment I felt totally, wantonly, his and could feel myself tensing for the delicious inevitability of coming against his relentless onslaught.

"Miss James?" The flight attendant soothingly cooed in my ear. "It's time to get that seat up now. We'll be landing at Shahjalal International Airport very shortly."

I had wanted the novelty of lingering in bed with my new lover. To spend the morning leisurely teasing and turning each other on and, when finally driven from my bed by hunger, perhaps a long post-coital get-to-know-you brunch at Luca's before spending the rest of the day in repeated performance. I had wanted to picture us as lovers, bonding over eggs and coffee, cautiously feeling each other out for signs that this might be more than just a one-night stand, secretly congratulating ourselves for having unexpectedly chosen someone we also wanted to spend time with. To enjoy in more than just a physical way, both of us relishing all those new and revelatory moments that happen only at the beginning of something. Instead, I had taken an early morning flight from JFK, endured a seemingly endless journey and stopover in Istanbul, and was now being expelled into the stifling heat and chaos of Bangladesh.

If I wasn't ready for this trip, I certainly wasn't ready for Dhaka. The hours spent in the subdued cocoon of the first-class cabin, with its succession of meals, drinks and bland movies really hadn't prepared me as I disembarked into the brilliant, blinding light and dazzling colors of the airport. Trying to navigate the swarming concourse to immigration seemed like a battle for survival, the airport alive with the press of people, most of whom were accompanied by excited children and makeshift boxes of luggage, food, clothes, imported television sets and electrical gadgets of all kinds. And noise—a cacophony of shouted greetings, pleas to dithering family members and the unintelligible P.A. announcements trying heroically to orchestrate the whole jumbled procession through the airport. Clutching my trusty Birkin and hiding behind my sunglasses, I felt carried along by the crowd until I noticed with relief a small sign with my name carefully written on it. The reassurance of seeing that familiar arrangement of letters cheered me, as did the smartly uniformed driver who promptly scooped up my bags and gestured towards the exit. Within minutes he had parted a determined way through the jostling crowds, whisked me through what otherwise looked like a lengthy and tedious immigration process, and ushered me into the welcome sanctuary of a waiting limousine.

It wasn't easy trying to relax on the drive into the city, and despite the jetlag and exhaustion, I could almost immediately feel a familiar sensation pulling at me. I couldn't deny the fact that I just loved this, the chaos and challenge of travel, the leaving behind of what's familiar, of what's easy. Of thinking in a different way, in a different language. All of it thrills me. I have gypsy blood. Even as a baby I would be dragged around the world with the rest of the family as my dad attended the seemingly endless global circuit of academic conferences and seminars and, despite everything, that first morning in Dhaka I could feel that recognizable sense of excitement stirring within me. Together with the rising anticipation of completing this assignment, there was the palpable excitement of beginning a new adventure, of being somewhere new, somewhere foreign, of being far away from what was accustomed and comfortable.

I thought at first there seemed little to distinguish Dhaka from so many other South Asian capitals I had visited. Even in the air-conditioned limo, the air became thick with the typical riot of foreign smells, where cooking smoke from a thousand street markets collided in a heady jumble with the oily stench of tuk-tuks. Yet as we moved through the interminable push of overcrowded buses, brightly colored tricycle rickshaws, scooters and ancient taxis all elbowing alongside each other, what did feel especially unique about Dhaka was its sheer sprawling size. It certainly felt like the most populous city on earth, and the press of hundreds of thousands of its people in its narrow and crowded streets felt palpable. As we drove gradually more slowly and deeper into the seething metropolis, it was also hard to miss the glaring chasm between the city's haves and have-nots. On one side of the road, the flimsy slums seemed to sprawl endlessly, overlooked on the other by the towering high-rises and gated residences of the city's well-to-do. Dominating everything else, I could feel the familiar sense of urgency that Dhaka shares with other eastern cities, the brash need for commerce, to exploit, to make money. To survive.

Once freed from the sluggish traffic, the car effortlessly navigated into the Bangladesh Diplomatic Zone picking up speed as we skirted the oily calm of Gulshan Lake and, a moment later, we were pulling into the lush garden driveway of the hotel. After the long flight, Dhaka's Grand Imperial was a particularly welcome sight, the ordered, managed cleanliness of the hotel banishing the chaos and clamor of the city outside its gates. Sprinklers hissed lazily over the manicured lawns and the air was heavy with the fragrance of hibiscus and clean wetness as the hotel staff hosed down walkways and gardeners expelled disorder from the rose beds. As I stepped out of the limousine, the entrance gleamed with shining brass reflecting the well-ordered bustle of an early morning luxury hotel. The sense of calm and formal hospitality enveloped me further as I crossed the lobby, my heels clicking on the cool marble, to the bows and whispered welcomes of the liveried bell staff, making me feel not like some travel-weary New Yorker but more like some kind of visiting dignitary or minor royalty.

At the reception desk, a smartly dressed clerk welcomed me, examined my passport, and passed me my room key.

"Oh, Miss James, you were expecting a visitor?" he asked, retrieving a business card and sliding it to me.

"I was?" I distractedly examined the card, hoping that this was a promising sign that the people I was here to meet would want to work quickly without all the usual bureaucratic red tape that often accompanied negotiations of this kind. But the owner of the card was not at all who I might have expected.

The clerk leaned a little closer and discreetly whispered, "The gentleman said he wished to wait, madame. He is seated in the Orchard Lounge just there." He pointed to a quiet seated area off of the reception lobby, overlooking the hotel gardens.

"And he asked for me?" I asked, puzzled.

"Yes, madame, by name."

As I made my way over to meet my guest, I could sense the fantasy of a stolen nap in clean sheets and the chance to sample room service evaporating, even as my curiosity sharpened.

It would have been hard to guess Jonathan Byrne's true age. His tanned, well-lined face suggested a long time spent in the East, perhaps in some diplomatic function, while his unruly, dirty-blond curls hinted at a single man, a career employee but with enough seniority to exercise his own sense of style. Even with all of that, he had a kind of old-world elegance about him and, sitting in an ivory linen suit, he looked every bit like a Graham Greene character, an image that only increased when I noticed the Panama hat in his hands when he rose to greet me.

"They give you people business cards these days, Mr. Byrne?"

"I like to be easily found when needed, Miss James," he smiled, stretching out his hand to take mine. Compared to his elegant attire, I was reminded of my own disheveled state after the long flight and, regretting that I hadn't freshened up before our meeting, took a seat across from him expectantly.

"May I offer you some refreshment—breakfast perhaps? I understand they're still serving by the pool." I caught a wistful glance toward the gardens.

"It's been a long flight from New York, Mr. Byrne. How about you tell me how I can help a representative from Interpol?"

"Of course, and my apologies, I'll get straight to the point. We understand you are here in Dhaka to conduct a transaction—the purchase of a particular artifact?"

The *we* bothered me, but it didn't seem he had asked a question he expected me to answer so I was relieved I didn't have to either confirm or deny it.

"The artifact in question has generated some interest by, let's just say, some of the more undesirable parties in this part of Asia," he continued. "And I'm here to extend to you any necessary protection during your stay here."

"I need protection, Mr. Byrne?"

He nodded thoughtfully. "You do. Absolutely, and I do want to make myself clear that this is an issue we believe extending far beyond just your own best's interests in the Dhaka. Our understanding is that there are others with an interest in your presence here and, as I say, they might be best described as perhaps not the most reputable sort of people."

I could easily detect an unmistakable Oxbridge accent tinged with something foreign and harder to trace, and despite his official formality, his blue eyes twinkled with something like concealed mischief. I was also just waiting for him to say "yes, quite" in that polite way, English people have of seemingly agreeing with you while at the same time suggesting that you have no idea what you're talking about."

"In my kind of work they seldom are," I smiled. "They're either rich, entitled and indifferent corporations or, when it comes to the antiquities market, obsessive academics, reckless treasure hunters... or worse."

"Yes, quite he said I don't doubt you must have encountered some colorful clientele in your line of work Miss James but I must impress upon you that we're not talking about the simple street must stands you may have heard of, this is organized crime on an unparalleled level. Think highly intelligent, well-funded criminal organizations capable of political corruption, murder, kidnapping...

That sort of thing." When he could see that I hadn't blinked, he pressed on.

The worst of them, a truly unpleasant character named Jai Khan, is considered something of a hero by his people in addition to being a millionaire several times over, but the fact remains that he and his kind are just ruthless tribal leaders of some quite fearsome organizations, well connected at every level and used to getting what they want. Right now, our intelligence suggests that what Jai Khan really wants is the Sarianidi Goddess."

Mention of the Goddess rattled me more than a little. The purpose of my trip was considered sensitive, recoveries of rare objects always are, and my clients at Bowden and Lowe had been very insistent on total discretion.

"You seem very well informed, Mr. Byrne," I said cautiously, stalling for time to think.

"What I know should worry you less than what others here in Bangladesh know," he said more urgently. "And it seems to be common knowledge that you've been authorized to release a large amount of money in exchange for the ...object in question."

"But I don't exactly carry it with me stuffed in a suitcase," I protested. "I'm an insurance-loss adjuster, Mr. Byrne. The most risk I encounter in my line of work is someone inadvertently moving the decimal point on a spreadsheet," I said, rising to leave. "Look, I appreciate your concern, I really do, but this time tomorrow I'll be on a flight back to New York, and I promise I'll do my very best to stay out of trouble until then."

He rose, too, exhaling a little too deeply as if trying to conceal his exasperation. "Well, quite, Miss James, that's really the problem now, isn't it? It is frankly more my concern that trouble will find you."

It wasn't the welcome to Dhaka I would have liked, and I had to admit to turning over in my mind the information I'd just been given, as a bellman found me and we took the elevator to the executive floor. I liked Byrne. He was obviously smart, had access to some good intelligence and seemed to genuinely care about my safety. And it also wasn't really unusual for me to encounter some branch of law enforcement when either investigating or trying to settle a claim. I'm never entirely at ease until I hand the check, or the insured property, to the client. But although I might have been concerned, I was also confident. In my experience I had rarely encountered any personal risks, particularly on a simple recovery assignment like this one. And although I'm very well paid to recover property, or provide compensation, for my clients, the tougher issues are usually confined to lengthy administration or tedious legal entanglements. Still, our brief conversation had left me a little unnerved and it was only when I had reached my room and dispatched the bellhop that I could close the door, kick off my heels and really digest what Byrne had told me. I suppose what bothered me the most was why the Sarianidi Goddess transaction had attracted the interest of a presumably senior Interpol officer, rather than warranting just a check in with the local police. The issue of security that Byrne had mentioned also gave me pause. It's usual protocol to have at least a personal bodyguard when traveling on a foreign assignment, yet my client had offered me none. Thinking I would be in Bangladesh for less than a day, and as a cursory check of the State Department website had shown no increased travel risk to the country, I was satisfied that I didn't need to take any additional precautions.

Playing the proposed deal over in my mind, I dismissed his fears, confident that this assignment didn't present any more significant threat than any other and that I would be able to conclude my business in Bangladesh quickly and easily.

Even with the memory of my very recent night of passion still fresh in my mind, I had a job to do and there are probably few things that excite me as much as throwing my bag into a new hotel room and with it, the anticipation of a whole new adventure. I reminded myself that I needed to make contact with my sellers at the auction house and complete any necessary verification, but my body felt sticky and tired and as I slid out of my clothes, I was fantasizing about the pleasure of a long shower and perhaps even the chance to re-live some more of my night with Scott. I stepped into the cool, beautifully appointed bathroom to turn on the shower and then everything went black.

I couldn't see, and I felt claustrophobic and nauseous, and when I came to, the pain in my left arm was excruciating, as if someone had punched it—and hard. Before I could totally gather my thoughts, I was aware of some kind of blindfold being removed and I found myself blinking in the light of a large, well-appointed and modern office. I immediately tried to focus on any details I could register, dumbly thinking this would be important when the police rescued me and would be pressing for vital information. I was on a high floor obviously, for as my eyes became used to the light, I could see the whole of Dhaka spread out before the expansive floor to ceiling windows. It was light, still the same day, or perhaps another day? The office was sparsely decorated in a tasteful, select way and the figure in front of me was speaking.

"My apologies for the nature of your arrival here, Miss James, it was an unavoidable means to attract your attention." I tried to focus on him, a tall, dark man standing in front of a long, beautifully carved desk, seemingly the only nod to traditional architecture in the otherwise sleeky appointed room.

"A phone call would have also worked," I managed to croak.

I suppose I was relieved that I wasn't tied to a chair in a grimy basement, dimly illuminated by the light of a naked lightbulb or something even more dramatic, but the mood in the room was still far from reassuring. As I got my bearings, I was aware of two other dark-suited men who lounged just outside my full field of view, behind me. It also bothered me that he obviously knew who I was. Even more alarming was that I seemed to be dressed only in a hotel bathrobe. The man speaking poured water from a glass carafe and offered it to me.

"Please, this might help," he said, with a concerned note that surprised me. This seemed more like some kind of nightmare boardroom meeting rather than the gloating of a maniacal kidnapper. I took the water gratefully, noticing powerful yet well-manicured hands.

"Although I would wish it otherwise, I'm afraid Bangladesh isn't always such a safe place for foreigners," he continued. "Particularly for those like you with, if I may say it, access to large amounts of money." His voice was oddly soothing, cultivated, with barely any trace of an accent. "I'd like to extend my protection until we can get you safely back on a flight home." This did not really seem like the approach of the kind of murderous gang lord I had been warned about by Byrne. But I had after all been drugged and kidnapped and didn't doubt I was in real danger.

"I'm afraid you'll have to get in line, Mr. ... ? I take it you're not Mr. Singh from the Municipal Auction House?"

A tight smile as he inclined his head and nodded.

"I've already been approached by a division of law enforcement also seemingly concerned about my security," I said. "A concern which I believe is exaggerated."

There was some low murmuring behind me at this news and although I had wanted to sound casual, I wanted my captors to know that there would be authorities looking for me. It might have been a risky move, but if an organization like this was as embedded as Byrne had led me to believe, they doubtless already knew anyway.

The man in front on me seemed quite unfazed by this news, but looked at me for a long moment before speaking. "Actually, I'm relieved that some measure of hospitality has already been extended to you, but I would remind you that you're alone in this city, and the reason for your visit has ... well, let's just say implications for a great many people."

"Well, I think my safety is really my own business," I said carefully. "As is my reason for being here in Bangladesh. It's just a simple transaction and I really can't see the wider implications for anyone in that." I was getting a headache and I although I had no idea who this guy was, or what he wanted, I really wanted to be out of that room. Having been in the city for such a short time, I was also getting tired of having exactly the same conversation with two different people.

He nodded, crossed the room to me and crouching to my eye level I thought for a frightening moment he was actually going to hit me. "Please don't be confused, Miss James, but the Sarianidi Goddess is very much my business also. I am, after all, the one you're here to meet."

"Then I have to disappoint you. I already have a fully negotiated agreement that I intend to honor with the original sellers," I said, with a boldness I felt evaporating by the second. My captor, if that's who this was, seemed intelligent, with a calm, authoritative and unflappable manner. I could easily understand why he might be the kind of leader others would want to follow. As I rapidly tried to pull myself into full consciousness, I could see he was dressed in a beautifully cut suit and tie, every bit the corporate titan with a sense of style, maybe even charm. Someone had tried, not totally unsuccessfully, to tame an unruly shock of black curls that hung over the collar of his crisp white shirt and it gave him the kind of shambolic chic that would have perhaps been better suited to a Bollywood movie star than a ruthless crime boss. He stood up and walked to the window, looking out over the city.

"Ah, yes, well, you should know there has been a very recent change of ownership of the Goddess," he continued smoothly.

"Am I then to understand that you are authorized to sell the artifact, legally?"

He turned back to me, smiling. "You seem overly concerned about my credentials, Miss James," he said sounding surprised and slightly amused.

"I'm interested only in art and the validity of those selling it, so please understand that I'm naturally curious about all those who share my interest, particularly those who apparently I'm to do business with."

"Then yes, we are the rightful owners of the object, and as I've stated, it is my intention that you shall return home with it as per your previous agreement. Think of it as a simple transaction with just slightly different players. If you would be so kind as to complete the necessary transactions from your end, I will arrange for the Goddess to be transferred to your safe keeping and you can leave—today if you wish. I can also guarantee you'll not be harmed."

"And yet evidence points to the contrary," I said rubbing my arm.

"Again, a necessary precaution to ensure your safety," Miss James.

"Drugging me and bringing me here against my will was to ensure my safety?"

"Dangerous times require drastic measures."

"And these are dangerous times?"

"You're an unaccompanied woman in Bangladesh, with authorized access to millions of U.S. dollars, information that seems common knowledge throughout Dhaka today—tell me, Miss James just how safe do you think you are?" He let that hang for a moment, his eyes dark and focused directly on mine, totally unreadable. "Now, perhaps you would be kind enough to share with me the exact arrangements for the transfer?" He was beginning to sound irked.

I hesitated for only a moment before I told him. "After I check the authenticity of both the artifact and the sellers, my buyers will send me the real-time banking instructions for the financial transaction and we'll conclude the agreement. As I've said, nothing can happen until the legitimacy of the sale is verified."

He nodded briskly. "Of course. I certainly appreciate that, but in that case, I'm sure you'll also appreciate the need for you to be our guest for a little longer." He signaled to the men behind me and I felt a brief pressure in my arm before everything went black. Again.

2 | SUAKA AWAN

When I came to, it wasn't entirely clear to me that I wasn't still dreaming. I was imagining a slender goddess dancing sensuously in front of me while through my hazy thoughts, the very air shimmered alive with the sound of tinkling temple bells, thick with exotic, unfamiliar scents. A cool breeze played over my naked body and as I opened my eyes, I found I was in a very luxurious bedroom, a large fan lazily revolving above me. Light was flooding in from open French doors and the sounds of birdsong, along with the heady fragrances of hibiscus, lilac and jasmine, filtered in from a garden beyond. As I shook off my drowsiness, I wasn't at all surprised to find there was indeed a beautiful woman in front of me.

"You're awake, Miss James," the woman said, smiling warmly.

She was tall, slender, indeterminably Asian, dressed in traditional loose black pants and a sleeveless vest revealing the golden-brown, toned skin of her arms and shoulders. Long, loose dark hair thickly framed her face with beautifully delicate features seasoned seemingly more from experience than age.

As I moved to get up from the bed, struggling to support myself, I felt that same punched in the arm feeling again from before. "Your boss has a nasty habit of drugging people," I grumbled.

"Not my boss actually, but apologies—you're in a very secure location now and it made sense that you should have no memory of your arrival here. The sedation should leave you pleasantly rested, no? The use and effect of drugs are something we understand very well here," she said without the slightest trace of irony.

And I couldn't actually argue with that. To my great relief I had no headache and, if anything, had a strangely pleasant feeling of being refreshed. Any feeling of jetlag I might have noticed landing in Dhaka had seemingly totally disappeared.

"And where exactly am I?"

"We call this place *Suaka Awan*, the Sanctuary of Clouds, as for exactly where that is, I think you know that's one question I can't answer for you," she admonished gently. "But you don't have to worry, you're quite safe here."

"So how come people keep saying they're so concerned about my safety, yet I keep being kidnapped?"

"Are you sure you're being kidnapped?" she asked.

"Aren't I?"

"It might help for you to think of this more as a refuge than a prison," she said, handing me a small glass of what looked like herbal tea. By the way she spoke, she was clearly no housemaid, nor the on-staff nurse to some criminal underworld gang. There was also the matter of her impressive physique. A guard perhaps? I wanted to test that theory.

"So, I'm free to go?"

"Anytime you wish," she said smoothly.

"I can just leave?"

"Of course. I'll just tell Jai Khan you were unsatisfied with the accommodations. I'm sure he wouldn't want to keep you against your will," she said, idly picking at an imaginary thread on the bed sheet.

"He's here?" The mention of that name again, and the fact that he might be here—wherever 'here" was—bothered me in a way I found surprising, but I shook off my curiosity. "Well then, I'd like to leave immediately," I said briskly as I uncertainly got to my feet and, grabbing the bed sheet around me, walked unsteadily to the balcony to get my bearings. I'm sure I must have gasped in shock when I realized the spacious patio opened up to a vast, uninterrupted view of endless, verdant jungle.

"I'll need a cab," I said with a confidence that was rapidly waning.

"Of course," she said stepping out onto the balcony behind me. "You'll find one, about two hundred miles that way." She pointed far across a long valley of undisturbed jungle. To my dismay there were no towns or even anything that looked like a settlement anywhere in sight.

"Just a word of caution, though," she added. "You'll probably need to cross the *Brahmaputra*. It's only half a mile wide at its narrowest, but the current is fierce and then there are the crocodiles and venomous water snakes." She shrugged casually. "Now, to the west, the jungle is impenetrable for a hundred miles, so south is probably your best bet, although it's tiger country and I'm told there's currently a man-eater patrolling in the region." She stepped back into the bedroom. "I'm sure you'll make out fine though," she said breezily.

"And north, let me guess?" I yelled back into the room.

"Oh, nothing, nothing really until you get to the Himalayas. I'd pack a sweater."

"I'm basically stuck here is what you're saying?" I glowered, following her back into the bedroom.

"Well, we're a long way from a taxi stand, or a Starbucks—or a police station if that's what you're thinking. There are no roads here, and the only way in or out is through the landing strip you came in on, but there are no planes here currently. You certainly have time to finish your tea," she said matter of factly.

"So I'm ..."

"Exactly!" she beamed, "our very honored guest, and I'm here to make your stay as comfortable as possible." It sounded like a speech from a hotel concierge, not what I took to be the bandit hostess of a jungle hideout, but it was said with such blatant honesty that somehow I didn't doubt the statement was genuine.

"My name is Aliyah, and I'm very pleased to meet you." Her smile was infectious and genuine. Her excellent English betrayed an Indochinese accent, highlighted with an unmistakable Western twang and, by her ease with idiomatic English, probably I guessed by way of somewhere like Berkeley or NYU. She radiated an easy confidence, yet beneath her charm her athletic body told me she could probably handle herself—and, more to the point, handle me, should she need to. I also wondered about the origin of a long and vicious scar down her left arm, the only feature that marred her otherwise impressive upper body. I sat back on the bed and absently sipped the tea.

"In that case I'd like to meet your boss. He has a lot of explaining to do," I said.

"Again, not my boss, but you do have an appointment with Jai Khan this evening and I'm sure he'll want to answer all your questions then," she replied. "Maybe first you'd like to freshen up—if you're up to it?"

"Sure, where is my luggage? I'll need my things," I said looking around the room anxiously.

"We have things," she said simply.

"My luggage, I need my luggage." I repeated.

"Why?" It seemed like a ridiculous question and I was momentarily stuck for an answer, but if I ever wanted to get out of here, my laptop and certainly my cellphone would be a start.

"I need my medication, I have a ... condition."

Aliyah's face clouded. "Please don't lie to me," she said evenly. "Let's be clear, Miss James, you are a guest here for reasons I'm honestly unaware of, and I believe I've convinced you that trying to leave would really not be in your best interest. You have questions, I understand that, and I'm sure they will all be answered, but in the meantime I suggest you rest, relax and everything will become clearer tonight. Now, how about a bath?"

I was aggravated, but at least the tea was helping calm me and she was reminding me that I had not bathed or washed my hair for, how long had it been—days?

Reluctantly I nodded, and she motioned me to follow her.

"Wait, I have no clothes," I said, realizing I was naked under the thin bed sheets.

"Come now, you have a remarkably beautiful body and you certainly have nothing to be ashamed of, Miss James. It was I, after all, who put you to bed."

Glaring even more, I wrapped the sheet tighter around me and hobbled behind her as she led me to a separate outside terrace where water was already filling a large pool. To describe it as a bath would be an injustice as it was at least half the size of my New York apartment. But in addition to its size, it was sunk into dark, gleaming hardwood flooring and overlooked stunning views of the surrounding jungle. In places, nature seemed to intrude into the structure of the terrace, and vines and artfully trained creepers wound into the roof and pillars. The trees seemed full of exotic bird calls and not far from the terrace I could hear a waterfall splashing soothingly to give the effect of some grove built into a precious yoga retreat. From this viewpoint I could also see that the whole structure was built into the side of a mountain, and while it felt secluded, cool refreshing breezes played over the terrace. I reflected that I had certainly stayed at luxury spas less well-appointed than this and when I dipped a toe into the water, it felt instantly inviting. Aliyah folded her arms and patiently watched me.

"You ... intend on staying?"

"Absolutely. Wouldn't have it any other way."

"I'm under surveillance?"

"Again ... "

"I know," I interrupted, "it's for my own fucking safety!"

Right, bitch, I thought and slipping the sheet off, stepped quickly into the bath. I had to admit, as it enveloped my whole body the water felt incredibly invigorating, scented I thought, with some kind of light herbal infusion.

To my astonishment, Aliyah quickly tied up her long hair, shed her clothes and slid in beside me.

"Wha ... ?"

"You need to be bathed and massaged. I'm sure your body has been through some trauma recently. Wouldn't it welcome some nourishment and love?" she soothed.

"I think I can manage," I protested, desperately trying not to conjure up exactly what "love" might mean. As if to answer she slipped behind me and, feeling her small breasts graze against my back and her long, limber arms encircle me, she gently leaned me back into the water.

"Shh, Miss James, by now you have doubtless convinced yourself that you are the guest of a dangerous and unpredictable man, and your very life might be in peril," she whispered conspiratorially, her lips grazing my ear. "Do you want to spend your last few hours worrying about your western ideas of nudity, or enjoying yourself? Think about it. The logic really is unarguable."

While there was nothing even slightly reassuring about her words, my protests quickly quietened. Her touch on me admittedly felt unbelievable, her strong hands intuitively finding my aching muscles and massaging them with a practiced skill. I found the weirdness about being washed by another person quickly dissolve as her practiced fingers worked my skin, easing and kneading my back and shoulders while unseen jets of water played over my body. Reaching for some kind of fragrant lotion, she lathered my hair and gently but firmly massaged my scalp, her fingers soothing and working attentively. Aliyah repositioned me slightly and I started as a particularly strong jet of water pulsed strategically against between my thighs. Whether it was the constant movement of water over me or Aliyah's strong hands and fingers doing such wondrous things to my body, I found myself becoming unexpectantly aroused. To my embarrassment, my body blatantly betrayed the effect with my nipples hardening visibly, my breathing becoming more conspicuous. She slid her hands between my legs and, resting on my pussy, seemed to artfully channel the relentless jets of water through her fingers to heighten the pulsing sensations against me. As I relaxed into the overwhelming sensitivity, I felt her lips softly grazing my neck and even as I murmured some kind of unintelligible protest, her fingers proved just as skillful and persuasive opening me up down there as they had been on my neck and shoulders. I felt myself quickly surrendering, my breathing quickening and my body blatantly bucking and writhing against her persistent caresses. I just didn't care anymore and my mouth hungrily found hers, her lips tasting sweet and wet. I could feel the pent-up stress since my arrival in Bangladesh and my bizarre abduction just dissolving under her careful attention and along with it, the frustrating need to come as she tilted my face more fully towards hers, and deeply kissed me, her tongue unhurriedly exploring mine. In contrast to my urgency, she was patient and thorough, and when it finally came, my orgasm was long, and yearning and desperate.

3 | JAI KHAN

"I'm not wearing that!" I said firmly.

Aliyah had draped a form-fitting red silk cheongsam across the bed. What little material there was seemed fashioned from almost liquid silk, the fabric elaborately embellished with chinoiserie toile gold dragons. More alarming still was that on one side, the dress was slit to the thigh, cut much higher than seemed decent.

"As you wish, but it's that or nothing. I'm afraid we had to burn your hotel robe, and to appear naked might send ... I don't know, the wrong message perhaps? He's only a man, you know."

"Wait a minute," I said thoughtfully. "Is this one of those weird cults where I'm kidnapped, then you're really nice to me and dress me up in strange clothes and then one day we commit some mass suicide ritual on the veranda?"

She laughed at this. "Well, I do practice yoga every morning on the veranda which can get a little out there sometimes, but I assure you, here this is considered entirely appropriate dinner attire."

I had already gotten over being naked in front of her, so I dutifully slid the dress over my hips, the material snugly hugging my breasts and thighs.

"And do I get shoes ... ?" I asked.

She shook her head, "I'll make a note next time to pop into our local Nordstrom's for you but for now, barefoot is fine here." She took a step back, and I felt her eyes drinking in my body in the form-fitting cheongsam. "You look beautiful, Brea," she sighed. "You better go before I eat you myself."

As she led me along a long rattan veranda, I had to admit the soft silk of the dress felt good next to my newly exfoliated and naked skin, particularly as I imagined I could still feel Aliyah's remarkable touch on my body beneath it. My little dalliance with her earlier had left no time for me to do anything more than gather my hair up in a messy chignon, and even though the air was cool in the compound, the traditional mandarin collar of the cheongsam seemed to only accentuate my bare neck, increasing the unfamiliar feeling of my growing vulnerability.

As we walked through the sprawling compound we passed storage rooms, spaces that looked like offices, a room of sophisticated electronic equipment (where the door was hurriedly closed as we passed) and various living quarters, all interspersed with outdoor spaces, splashy fountains and breezy corridors. Further down the walkway the corridor opened out into a large dining area and Aliyah indicated through a set of large doors leading off to another secluded veranda.

"Bon appetite," she grinned and disappeared into the maze of the compound.

Although he looked less formal than at our first meeting, the suit replaced with faded jeans and a crisp white dress shirt, Jai Khan still exuded that conspicuous, almost calming sense of overwhelming authority. I watched him for a moment as he sat, studying the fading sunset before he saw me approach and leapt up, beaming a white and unforced smile.

"Miss James, you look refreshed and I must say, already perhaps a little more relaxed."

Unashamedly surveying my body accentuated by the thin, tight silk, he extended his hand. "Please let me properly introduce myself. I am Jai Khan," he announced. I declined my hand yet sensed again that unfamiliar feeling of powerlessness, of vulnerability. I also felt an overwhelming, simmering resentment.

"I am an American citizen, and you, Mr. Khan, are in a shitload of trouble."

"It would not be for the first time," he said, still smiling and holding up his hands defensively.

"Please ..." He indicated a long comfortable-looking couch that I immediately realized would pose an interesting challenge in the figure-hugging short dress.

"I have a nasty feeling I'm going to be blindfolded again."

"Oh, only if you really wish to be," he laughed, seemingly delighted. "Ah but yes, that dry sense of humor again! I believe that's so unusual in the art world."

"I must remember to add it to my resume," I said.

"You should, really, but I did want to see you, to apologize for earlier. There were some pressing things I needed to accomplish while in Dhaka, and time was of the essence ... "

He paused as an attendant, resplendent in a crisp white jacket, arrived from nowhere, offering me an ice-cold drink.

"I realize I was less than gracious on our first meeting, and I'd very much like to make amends for that." He indicated to the tray and I must have raised my eyebrows as he hastily explained.

"A Spanish gin and tonic in a tall glass and believe me, honestly, otherwise untouched and singularly lacking in sedatives."

"You ... you've researched my beverage preferences?" I asked, incredulous.

He shrugged, "Instagram, whatever ... you know, I have ... people." He waved vaguely.

"Oh, I'm sure you do." I muttered under my breath.

I took a sip of my drink and had to admit it was perfectly mixed, the bittersweet flavor of the tonic mingling with the bright citrusy tang of the alcohol perfectly hitting the spot. I permitted myself to take in the view for a moment, a stunning panorama over the long valley, thick with vegetation now tinged with gold in the setting sun. Far in the distance and reflecting the fading sunlight, I caught a glimmer of what I thought must be the river Aliyah had mentioned. Although impenetrable and intimidating, I had to admit my prison was not without beauty. There was a surprisingly easy silence between us as Khan let me drink in the spectacular view.

"So, what exactly am I doing here, Mr. Khan? What is it you want from me?" I asked eventually.

"Ah, yes of course," he leaned closer. Clearly, he was more of a conversationalist than our first meeting had suggested. "There have been complications, I'm afraid. Not on my side, and surely not ones I hadn't anticipated, I must say, but still they might require my attention ... and more time perhaps. A little more patience." I had remembered the intensity of his eyes from the brief interrogation in his office at Dhaka, but here they never left my face for a second, contrasting against his dark skin and equally as mesmerizing as the intensity with which he spoke.

"Complications?" I queried.

"Yes, the previous seller of the Goddess was anxious to offload the piece quickly and, if I might say so, without due consideration. Consequently, the asking price was paltry. You understand these kinds of negotiations better than I, Miss James, but suffice for us to say it was substantially below actual market value. We are currently negotiating for a more appropriate sum, a process that might take some time."

I struggled to contain some rising anger.

"Perhaps you're not aware that I'm the only one authorized to broker a deal like that, particularly at, I'm assuming, a now greatly inflated asking price?"

"Quite so, Miss James, and believe me I would much have preferred to negotiate with you—I don't doubt your skills are quite impressive—but sadly the nature of our arrangements require other channels to conclude the sale." If he saw my face darken, he added hastily, "Of course, you will be in a position to confirm the final arrangements and, when resolved satisfactorily by all parties, the artifact will be safety surrendered to your possession."

I was tempted to use the "we don't negotiate with terrorists," line but instead asked, "And this requires me being forcibly taken and detained here?"

"Again, I can only ask your understanding in this. I agree I have behaved abominably, but please believe me, there are other players with an interest in our transaction with methods far worse than mine. Here in the East, we have been trading for centuries. I even dare to believe we're rather good at it, yet your Western concepts of right and wrong and fair play are quite foreign here. If I've seemed at all heavy handed to you, it's only because I've had to be. Once they had got what they wanted, believe me these other interests would not care so much about your wellbeing."

I wasn't too sure what to make of this at all. I could understand that Khan wanted me out of the way to negotiate his own, no doubt dishonest, deal. As Johnathan Byrne had warned on my arrival in Dhaka, Khan also seemed to be implying there were other criminal elements who also knew about the Goddess and somehow wanted in on the deal. I sipped more of the cooling drink, savoring the reviving mixture of cardamom and juniper and tried to return to the point.

"What you've described so far sounds like extortion to me, Mr. Khan, and, as I tried to explain to you before, it would make any deal with my buyers invalid. There's also the point about my kidnapping, and as far as I'm aware those are crimes pretty much everywhere."

He shrugged, "As I've said, the rules here are perhaps a little different, but I don't want to add to my crimes by being guilty of being a terrible host, so please, come—you must be starving, will you eat?"

"No, absolutely not." I had already decided that I wouldn't be cooperating with my captors in any way. The incident earlier in the pool with the girl had clearly been a mistake, one that I could explain away by being exhausted, stressed and perhaps even still under the influence of whatever sedatives were still running around in my system, but I certainly wasn't going to eat with this man, no matter how charming he might seem.

"What I would like, Mr. Khan, is to be taken back to my hotel."

"You're not comfortable here?" he seemed genuinely confused.

"I'm sure you people think you can deceive me into agreeing to some highly illicit deal by hiding me away in this phony jungle resort and killing me with kindness. Since I've arrived here, I've been bathed by some no doubt psychopathic girl, been given clothes that make me look like a hooker and offered cocktails that probably contain who knows what and I want it to stop, immediately!"

I wondered if I may have gone too far. For a moment I couldn't interpret the look on his face. Was he about to hit me or burst out laughing?

"My staff tell me we have a basement here that is freezing cold at night and stifling with the daytime heat. I believe it may also have rats," he said calmly. "If it would sit more favorably with your conscience, I could arrange for you to be moved there, but please make no mistake, Miss James, you will be staying here until this transaction is concluded." He waited, letting that sink in before he suddenly smiled again and rose, beckoning me to join him.

"You have a reputation as a talented negotiator, Miss James. Your clients would not have retained you for this assignment were you not. Why not join me for dinner and we can, at least ... negotiate?"

I was seething at the arrogance of this man. Even more shocking to me was the realization that I had now had absolutely no control of anything anymore. Not the purchase of the Sarianidi Goddess, the opportunity for any access to my clients, or even my personal safety—nothing was guaranteed anymore. I was totally and clearly on my own. I drained my glass in one swallow and felt myself follow him, at the same time hating myself for doing so. Worse still, as he led me back into the long dining room, I felt my loathing, along with my resolve, instantly weaken. He had led me into a vaulted great room designed in a characteristically indigenous style, with an impressive timber construction supporting an airy roof structure. It was decorated in a blended Eastern style with tasteful mixtures of Indian and Arabic design; large candles had been placed in heavy glass hurricanes lighting an immense, dark wood table that was being covered with plates of delicious looking food. Khan seated me in a surprisingly gentlemanly, almost old-fashioned way, then poured wine for us both.

"You're not a Muslim, or a Hindu, Mr. Khan?"

"I'm neither ... and maybe all," he said. "And please, call me Jai."

"A man without religion? No wonder you lack any moral code," I admonished, perhaps more harshly than I had intended.

He laughed at my barb, shaking his head as he sat across from me. "Well, as you might know, the history of man cultivating grapes was first recorded in my part of the world. I don't recall anyone being too upset with it at the time. And as for religion, I am a man without a lot of things," he said. For a moment, I thought I detected a tinge of regret in his voice. Was this remorse, loss? Something I couldn't fathom. Eyeing the beautiful dining room and the sumptuous feast before us I muttered, "Somehow I doubt that."

He caught my arm, but gently, and looked intently into my eyes.

"I don't know where it is written that a man can't be successful, but please understand this, I can only make money when *everyone* is making money. Poverty, corruption, ignorance—none of these things are very good for business."

"Trickle up versus trickle down? That's very noble of you."

"Exactly, Miss James. And you may be correct I am a capitalist, not a charity, but that's not to say there's no room for a little altruism along the way. I would also admit to being no saint by any stretch of the imagination, but these are my people after all, and how I get to lead them, if I ever get to achieve that, may well be at odds with your ideas of democracy. What is it your people say about a rising tide? I'd like to be the one who will help raise these people."

"And that's very admirable of you, Mr. Khan. I'm assuming the murdering, extortion and —here I'm taking a wild guess—drug pushing are all part of that process of raising your people?"

"Oh, how you underestimate me!" he laughed again. "There's also the software piracy and shady real estate and property interests you need to consider, although, and despite their obvious financial benefits, I have to confess to disowning the heroin trade and, come to that, also human trafficking and prostitution. I know you have a low opinion of me and, as I said, you might be right, but perhaps we'll have to agree to disagree on our ethical positions," he said as if to close the subject. "Now then, shall we eat?"

Across the table I think Khan could see the defiance in my eyes, and he sighed, looking again at me directly with a surprising intensity. "Here it is the custom to share food, even with one's enemies. The thought is that by sharing food we might perhaps come together a little, maybe even resolve some of our differences?" He tapped the sides of a large copper bowl between us. "*Shanwari*, it is a specialty from the region where I was born and really is quite delicious, you must try it," he urged. The wonderful aromas were admittedly driving me crazy and I was aware of a gnawing hunger in my stomach that I wasn't sure I could ignore any further.

"It doesn't mean I'm complying or that I'm agreeing to anything—just so we're clear," I sniffed.

"Absolutely clear," he nodded.

He peeled off a piece of warm bread and showed me how to scoop the meat. Maybe it was because I was starving, or maybe it was the alcohol, but the food was delicious and with each bite I felt my resolve melting further away. Although I still felt uneasy about enjoying his hospitality so much, being in his company somehow felt intimate, and for a man who had drugged me twice and whisked me away to who knows where, he also had the reassuring effect of making me feel weirdly safe. He was attentive and charming and, in equal measure, funny and thoughtful, and as he guided me through a host of unrecognizable dishes, I found myself forgetting that I was actually being held prisoner by these people, a guest of terrorists.

"You said you were renegotiating the price? Yet you live like a man who doesn't need money."

"On the contrary there is never enough for the work I want to do, for what I know can be achieved."

"Which is what exactly?"

"Education, for a start—and particularly for girls and women. Where there is so much poverty, education is the only way out, the hope that holds for millions of people. We urgently need improved healthcare, better security, stronger, more informed leadership; all of that comes from education."

"Admirable goals, I'm sure. And is Aliyah one of the women benefiting from your largesse?"

The atmosphere in the room changed immediately, and when he looked at me, this time his gaze was cold and forbidding. "I would strongly suggest that's an accusation you don't share with her," he said slowly. "Aliyah had been a guest of the Taliban when I raided one of their camps some years ago. I will confess that for one so young she had the kind of hatred in her soul which, to my discredit, has been useful to my organization at times. She is very dear to me, but no, if that is your question, Miss James, she is not my mistress, not my project."

"I apologize, that must have been horrible for her, I just meant ... "

He held up his hand. "No need, Miss James. I assure you she later found her captors and ended their lives in a way I hesitate to describe to you while we are at table."

I must have slightly shivered at the thought of what had happened earlier in the pool, and the uncomfortable fact that my latest lover might also have been an efficient and vengeful killer, but I was also trying to keep Khan on track.

"But if you're the patriot you say you are, wouldn't you want the Goddess to remain in your own country?"

He fell silent for a moment before answering. "Would I not prefer the Goddess to remain where she belongs? Well yes, yes, I dearly would. But her presence won't feed people, educate children or overthrow our currently corrupt and tyrannical regime, Miss James. Yes, of course, I would prefer the Sarianidi Goddess to stay in our country in the same way I wish that we were not so reliant on money from other countries to feed and educate our children, or foreign interests to be responsible for our own safekeeping. But now is not the time for wishing. At the moment the statue is useful only in its utility."

"I'm shocked to hear you say that. Do you even know the first thing about the Goddess?"

"Do I?" He seemed amused again, a glint returning to his eyes as if he was playing with me. "Let me see now, she is, I seem to recall, a Bactrian figurine that disappeared from Afghanistan's Kabul National Museum in 2001, named after the man who excavated it, a Soviet archeologist by the name of Viktor Sarianidi." He took a sip of wine. "You'll recall at the time the Taliban were busy trying to destroy every museum artifact that they could find—anything that bore a human or animal likeness—so it is believed that the Goddess was hidden, maybe even lost. Another story suggests she may have been hastily sold to raise funds for the removal and safe keeping of some of the museum's larger, more culturally impressive exhibits. In any event, she completely disappeared."

"Until now."

"Until now," He continued. "The statue recently came into the possession of a former official at the museum, was then sold on the black market to a buyer in Kandahar, and then onto Bangladesh. I am in the fortunate position of being able to relieve it from its last owner."

"I understand the symbolic meaning of the Goddess exceeds even its auction price?" I asked.

He nodded. "I don't think anyone alive today truly understands the significance of the figurine, some believe she was an elite member of Bactarian society or maybe a fertility fetish, while others consider her a deity—a Goddess. In any event her value to culture, to my people is beyond value."

"That's an impressive review, Mr. Khan."

He bowed, "Perhaps we have a different association with our history than you do in the United States," he said, and I thought I almost detected him blush.

"You say that you are in the position to 'relieve' it from my original seller? I take it you'll have the necessary documents reflecting the transfer to your possession?" I pressed.

"This is currently in progress as we speak, and is the only reason I would ask you to remain with us." I felt an urgent need to contact someone at Bowden and Lowe to find out if this increasingly complicated deal was even still on.

The conversation over dinner had felt light and surprisingly enjoyable. Occasionally we'd spar on some issue, or I would sense him testing me on some topic or another, but he had quieted the hostility I had felt earlier with an ease that amazed me and the evening swept by quickly and surprisingly effortlessly. By the time we had eaten our fill, I was aware of an odd and strangely persistent feeling that made me think for a moment that perhaps I *had* been drugged again. The wine had certainly gone to my head and I was sure that traces of the recent sedations were probably still in my body. But mostly I was feeling oddly turned on by hearing this stranger talk. There was something attractive about his passion and his genuine conviction. It felt reassuring, and even sexy, and I was aware of how closely I was leaning as he talked.

"I feel I've bored you long enough, Miss James," he said suddenly, as if reading my thoughts. "I should let you get some rest, but I've very much appreciated your company and although the thought might seem disagreeable to you, I'd like you to think of yourself as my guest. If there is anything you should need during your obligatory stay with us, I know you'll be in good hands with Aliyah."

I wondered briefly if he was aware of my little assignation with her earlier, but I was sure there was probably little he didn't know, particularly in his own house. Getting up from the table, he wished me a good night and turned to leave me.

"I might not understand your ways, or your customs, but you do understand it's wrong to keep me here?" I ventured as a parting shot.

He turned to face me, hesitating with a quizzical look on his face. "Wrong?" He seemed genuinely confused. "Are you always so sure what's right and wrong, Miss James?"

"It's usually pretty obvious to me, Mr. Khan. Yes, I've got to say I do."

"In that case, I envy you. To have that kind of certainty must truly be reassuring. You are indeed a most fortunate woman." He stood there for a moment looking at me as he had the first time we met, as if weighing something else, then he wished me goodnight again, his voice now formal again after the easy intimacy that had marked our dinner, and left.

Without his presence I suddenly felt even smaller in the massive dining room. His charisma was all embracing, engaging and somehow fascinating to me. I felt myself almost immediately fighting the conflicted feeling of both loathing and missing him at the same time. This was my captor, a killer, a criminal, a terrorist—hadn't Jonathan Byrne told me as much? And yet, he was charming and intelligent, bringing me into his world without excuse or shame. I sat there feeling suddenly and utterly alone, not just feeling Jai Khan's absence but also not really trusting my own feelings. In the few hours I had been held captive here, and despite my better instincts, both the Aliyah and now Jai Kahn had done everything to persuade me that I wasn't in any danger. I truly didn't know what to think or what the next move would be. Coming from my controlled, well-ordered life, I found that not knowing more than just unsettling. As I played with the last swallow of wine, realizing just how terrified I felt, I wondered how long I would be required to be a prisoner here and how this might all end. A short while later, attendants soundlessly cleared the remains of our feast, leaving me alone in that absurdly romantic setting

I awoke the next morning to a cacophony of jungle sounds. It was curious that even with the bizarre events of the day before still fresh in my mind, I didn't wake in confusion or panicked about where I was. Instead, I felt only a refreshing sense of calm as I listened to the call of birds and chatter of monkeys outside my window. Someone had placed a short kimono-style robe on my bed, and wrapping it around me, I cautiously explored the compound. Padding quietly around the waking building, I was again captivated by the magic of the place. As prisons go, *Suaka Awan* was hard to fault and as I explored the sprawling complex, workers in the house smiled and acknowledged me as if I were a guest at a swanky resort. The structure itself was impressively built in the traditional style and was much larger than I had originally thought. A series of wide, thatched roofs covered the entire compound, with the main public rooms grouped around a central courtyard. Here a large fountain lazily bubbled into pools of silently gliding Koi, water plants and ornamental grasses. Long, airy corridors led to other, secluded courtyards deeper within the complex where smaller water features cooled the air and completed the general air of tranquility. Cut into the valley sides there was even a swimming pool, fed by the waterfall I had heard earlier. The rooms themselves all seemed luxurious, the largest being the great room where I had dined with Jai Khan last night, while all of the outer rooms presented wraparound balconies in a colonial style. The surrounding views from every aspect were of thick impenetrable jungle. Aliyah hadn't exaggerated the remoteness of the compound, and although there seemed to be a small staff, she was, of course, quite right; there was little stopping me escaping. The door to my room was not locked; there were no apparent guards. It crossed my mind that there would probably be cameras following me, but if so they were well disguised. As if by magic, towards the end of my exploration, she appeared out of nowhere.

"Well, good morning Brea, how was your dinner?"

"It was ... fine."

She studied me expectantly as if waiting for me to add more detail, but I truthfully didn't know what I thought about Jai Khan and last night's dinner conversation. "It's just that ... "

"That it's a lot, right?" she finished my sentence.

"Yes, I'm still trying to get over the idea that I didn't ... dream any of this."

"No. No you didn't. You are, temporarily, here with us and you will soon be back in America with what you came for." Sensing the silence, she asked, "Hey, ever tried Javanese coffee—real Javanese?" When I shook my head, she grazed my hand and beckoned me follow her to one of the interior shady poolside areas. In further evidence of her hostess skills, a silver salver of breakfast things had already been prepared on a café table by some comfortable looking couches.

"This is *toraja;* it's from South Sulawesi," she said pouring the coffee, "and it's not easy to find but I always try to stash some here."

"You live pretty well for outlaws," I said, settling down next to her and thinking back to last night's feast.

She shrugged, "I know you think of this place as a prison, but to us it's a refuge, a place to recharge, to escape."

"Escape from what?"

"We have enemies. I'm sure you've realized by now—rivals, unfriendly governments, people who see Jai Khan and what he stands for as an obstacle to getting what *they* want. It's good to have place where, well, we hope no one will look."

"What he stands for?"

"I can't believe you survived an entire dinner with him without him telling you his plan for saving the world," she laughed. Remembering the conversation over dinner, I did recall his conviction and the intensity with how he described a better, a brighter, future for his country as a whole. None of it typical gangster rhetoric I had to agree.

"Sounds like you don't particularly share his views?"

She shrugged. "He's my friend, a good man, an honest one, too, and believe me it's hard to find either around here. He believes he's trying to do the right thing and I'm here simply because I owe him my life. Politics interest me less than trying to stay alive."

"But why here, why this place? From what he told me last night, you're all so far from home."

"When you come from nowhere, you can *be* anywhere I guess," she said enigmatically. "And this part of the world became popular after the wars and insurgencies, you know? Afghanistan, Iraq and Syria..

"Jai Khan is from there?" I pressed.

She shook her head. "Jai Khan comes from a country that doesn't even exist anymore so you'll give yourself a headache trying to figure out where he comes from. The thing is he's learned to be rootless; he operates across a pretty wide territory," she said it as if he were no more than an area manager of a suburban real estate company.

"Hence a remote place like this."

"Exactly, yes. Here we're in the middle of nowhere but kind of at the crossroads to everything—the Gulf States and Africa, Asia, China—we're surrounded by big markets where there's money to be made." I was beginning to understand that she had a very casual way of imparting important information. If there was any meaning or motive behind it, she had a way of letting me decide.

"Here try this, it will wake you up." She passed me a cup of the beautifully aromatic coffee as if to change the subject.

"So how about you? Where are you from?"

"I'm Malay, or that's what I considered myself a long time ago."

"I heard how you came to be here with Jai. I'm sorry."

"It was a long time ago," she waved off my sympathy dismissively, "My father was an engineer working for the government in Afghanistan. When they, the Taliban, rose to power, he was arrested one day simply for being a foreigner, for trying to improve the country. The next day they came for my mother and me."

"I don't know what to say, I'm just so sorry."

She shrugged. "I guess there is such a thing as being in the wrong place at the wrong time—it seems to happen to me a lot," she almost laughed, but then I sensed her bristle. "But I don't need sympathy, Brea, I won't let anyone think of me as just a victim of human slavery, as someone who's just prepared to suffer the consequences of that." Her eyes danced and there was an almost imperceptible hardening to her voice. "When this all goes south—and it most certainly will, because history has a harsh way of treating people like Jai and I—I'll be okay. When you've been forced to learn how to survive, sooner or later you become really good at it, so let us be quite clear, Brea, of the two of us, I'm really not the one who need rescuing."

"Ah ha, so you agree, I do need rescuing," I shot back.

"I believe you believe that," she said, the calm now returned to her voice. "But if I were you, I would think that this is actually the safest place for you right now."

"Doesn't it bother you that I may be killed, murdered?"

"Yes, that troubles me greatly, particularly now I know how good your pussy tastes," she giggled into her coffee cup trying to hide her smile, and the iciness was broken.

"Then you won't help me to escape?"

"If you're still assuming it's safer for you out there than here," she said more calmly, "that's really not what I've heard."

"What *have* you heard?" I asked, immediately curious.

"Maybe it's about your statue, the Goddess, Brea. It seems to be much more than some dusty artifact, more like a ... I don't know, a key? A pawn that everyone seems to want right now. It's part of a bigger puzzle, something bigger than you."

"Something bigger than Jai?"

"I would let Jai look after Jai and, by the way, if it's any consolation Jai Khan is a businessman above all. Killing people doesn't make for good business—it's counterproductive and messy. There's no reason why you shouldn't leave here alive."

"Well, that's fucking reassuring," I laughed.

I contemplated this as I savored the coffee for a moment and, of course, Aliyah was right, the lush taste of caramel and chocolate combined perfectly with its reviving sharpness. I don't think I had ever tasted anything quite like it.

"What did you mean about Jai Khan coming from a country that doesn't exist?" I asked.

"His ancestral home—and here you can bet people trace their family lines back a thousand years—was carved up by the superpowers long ago. His family was displaced and then ruled by a succession of crackpots, despots and religious freaks. When I first met him, he was a warlord. Not your typical warlord, I'll admit, but nonetheless a leader of people, and he's been fighting ever since."

"So where does his reputation as a gang leader come from?"

"That depends on who's writing the history doesn't it?" she signed. "Terrorist, freedom fighter, patriot, businessman, thief ... ? But so many questions, Brea. You're not revising your idea of him as a despicable, criminal terrorist are you?" she teased.

"I'm sure he's a lot of things, and even he doesn't deny many of them, but there's ... I don't know," I sensed her watching me playfully.

"Tsk, tsk, Brea, am I really not enough for you?" she pouted.

"About that ..." I began. "I'm not really sure what happened yesterday between us but that's not me, I mean, I just don't behave like that. I wouldn't want you to think I'm ..."

"What, a lesbian? Neither am I." She put down her coffee cup and looked at me intently. "Listen, the world is violent and cruel and unfair, and it could end for us at any moment. Taking pleasure, taking comfort where we can, that should be enough for you—for any of us." She leaned over and gently pushed a strand of hair off my face, her easy familiarity again shocking me.

"You'll be okay; this will end. In a few days you'll be back in America and none of this will matter. Our lives are so separate; maybe we should just enjoy it when they come together."

No matter how welcoming these people seemed, I still wasn't convinced and spent the rest of the day convincing myself that I needed to escape. Clearly, I didn't belong here in a terrorist stronghold and even the thought of what these pleasant, hospitable people might also be capable of made me shiver. Beneath his charm, I had no doubts that Jai Khan was a dangerous man, and my conversations with both he and Aliyah had done nothing to dispel the idea that these were, in fact, hardened criminals.

I had seen the river from the balcony before dinner last night and reasoned that where there was a river there would be boats, settlements—who knows—eventually even a road that could lead me back to civilization and the authorities? Despite being their prisoner, I wasn't sure that I wished Jai Khan and his band any harm but staying here just wasn't an option. I wanted to do my job, complete my assignment and go home with my hard-earned commission. None of that was going to happen languishing in some jungle retreat.

I didn't see either Aliyah or Jai Khan for the rest of the day, and after an orderly arrived at noon to serve me lunch on a tray, I tried to evaluate my escape plan. The skies had been so clear the previous night I felt I could easily navigate by the moon. It was also a sign of my captor's casual confidence that I had even discovered a sharp knife in the fruit bowl in my room. Otherwise, my jungle preparedness was sorely lacking. I had no protection against insect bites, no real weapon or even a machete to help me hack my way to the river. My wardrobe was also wildly inappropriate, consisted of a variety of sarongs, a too-small T-shirt borrowed from Aliyah, a swimsuit (also hers) and a wide-brimmed straw hat donated from the kitchen staff. I had finally been given sandals to wear around the compound although I longed for my trusty Reeboks, which as far as I knew, were still unpacked in my suitcase at the hotel. I felt absurdly under prepared and not at all confident, but I also felt it was now or never.

As soon darkness fell, I made my escape and it was easier than I thought. If there were no guards, maybe there were no cameras either and I saw no one as I stepped out to my balcony. The front of the compound was raised high above the valley floor supported by tall wooden pillars, and a quick glance earlier had confirmed it would be a dizzying drop to the ground. However, at the back, where most of the sleeping quarters were, the structure was much closer to the ground, raised only twenty or thirty feet. I slipped easily over the balcony, shimmied down the wide supporting beams and jumped the last few feet to the ground. In less than a minute I was safely on the jungle floor. I felt almost cheated that my daring escape hadn't involved knotted bedsheets or evading armed guards and probing searchlights. My captors had been complacent and had greatly underestimated my craving for freedom; it had been as unexpectantly easy as that. I was free and headed towards the river.

"It was the spiders wasn't it?"

A shadow separated itself from the darkness, but the voice was instantly familiar.

" ... because I distinctly remember telling you about the snakes, the tigers and all the other dangers the jungle offers, but if I'd just told you about the spiders, and particularly what a neuro-toxin bite can do to you—how you're slowly, painfully paralyzed even before the delirium starts to kick in, and all of this a long time before you finally get to die—if I had only mentioned that, then of course I wouldn't have found you wandering around in the jungle this evening, would I? You would have done as you were told and stayed put in the building."

"Fuck!"

"Love to, but seriously this isn't the place. The whole thing with the spiders ... " she mimicked horror. Aliyah looked relaxed, hands by her side. For one ludicrous moment I wondered if I could rush her, before remembering Jai Khan's cautionary story about how she had dealt with her Taliban abductors. I was already tired, sweating and foot sore, and it felt as if I had been pushing my way through the thick jungle undergrowth for several hours since leaving the compound, yet here she was, calmly in my path and I wasn't sure what would happen next.

"Are you going to let me go?" I asked, testing her.

"I think I already told you that I wouldn't stop you."

"Then?"

"I'm just curious about *where* you're going?"

"I'm a prisoner. You know that and I also think you know that it's wrong. Can't you just tell Jai Khan you didn't know I was gone until morning?" I pleaded.

I sensed, rather than saw, her smile in the darkness.

"I think you know I'm not going to do that, Brea."

"But you're not going to stop me either?"

47

"Maybe I won't have to," she said simply. "If you're as smart as I think you are, you'll rethink your little walk in the woods. You must know that you'll be dead, or will at least have contracted malaria or a whole menu of other tropical fevers in a day or two anyway. You'll never find the river, or get anywhere near it. You'll wander around in circles. Your body will never be found. The ants will pick clean what the bigger animals didn't finish."

"I'll take my chances." I said, less certainly.

She shrugged. "Okay, go. Go and die. It really makes no difference to me. But before you do, you should maybe know just one thing." She took a step closer and I noticed her amused glance at the fruit knife I had been clutching since I jumped off the building.

"Before you arrived in Dhaka, Jai learned there was word among the street gangs, the *mastaans*, that an unescorted American girl was arriving who had access to a great deal of money. We know you were followed from the airport, and our guess is they planned either to hold you for ransom or, even though they had no chance of getting the Goddess, to use you to extort money from your buyers. Either way you would have probably ended up dead in a Dhaka alley or worse, maybe sold into slavery. Jai thought you might prefer his hospitality, at least until he had negotiated the sale of the Goddess. It would give his deal some legitimacy, you could return with the Goddess and there would be no unnecessary bloodshed."

Hearing this made me think about what he had said about other interests, other players, the night before.

"It's in his interest to keep me safe?" I found myself saying aloud.

"I'm just saying, Brea—but it's okay, please just go ahead and do what you have to do. Go die in some foreign jungle for a reason you haven't yet bothered to think through. Make some pointless, fruitless sacrifice for absolutely no reason at all."

We stood there in the shadow of the clearing, two women from opposite sides of the earth, facing each other with the sounds of the jungle surrounding us.

"Or you can come back with me, be safe until it's time for you to return. And I promise you *will* be safe."

She turned her back on me and headed back to the compound, muttering loudly to herself as she left. "Oh, by the way, the chef's preparing *Bakso* tonight, not that you're interested, but you'll be missing a treat. Anyway, we'll be thinking of you, out here in the jungle. Lost. Alone," she taunted. "It's been lovely knowing you, Brea James."

I stood alone in the darkness watching her go, and after a moment's hesitation, reluctantly followed her. I had gone a dozen paces before I realized that the structure of the compound was looming right in front of me. Aliyah had been right, since my escape I had done nothing but walk in circles.

I wasn't too sure how I felt about a notorious tribal outlaw being a knight in shining armor, particularly *my* knight, as a person he hadn't met before or had any interest in. As things had proven, he could push the sale of the artifact quite easily without me, although Aliyah was right, there was no earthy reason why he would want me dead and it might even be useful to him that I was kept alive.

One day at the compound turned into several days, and simply because there was nothing else to do, I found myself relaxing into my prison surroundings to pass the time. Among the other facilities the compound offered I was amazed to discover a beautiful and extensive library. If I was surprised at all about the inclusion of a library in this remote hideout, I was even more surprised by its extensive contents. Books covering everything from American politics to eastern philosophy lined the shelves. Here I discovered Rousseau rubbing shoulders with Keynes, Adam Smith with Mandela, Kant with Sun Tzu. There was poetry, too: Sappho, Shakespeare's sonnets and Whitman, and organized stacks of faded periodicals and newspapers, *The Guardian, The New York Times, Al Sabah Al Jadid* and a dozen more in Turkish, Urdu and Arabic. More surprising still was the discovery of a computer that I was allowed to use, although I quickly found a blocking program prevented me from using email or any external communication.

Since our dinner, I had seen little of Jai Khan, other than coming across him somewhere in the complex, usually talking on several different phones or giving instructions to his staff. He seemed impressively multilingual, speaking Arabic to his associates, Pashtu or Bangla to the compound staff and, when with Aliyah, he would speak either English or something light and lyrical I couldn't place, almost like Lao or Thai. Whenever I ran into him I felt the disquieting sensation of feeling foolish and unprepared, wanting somehow to impress him, as if I was back at high school and he was a boy I had some ridiculous crush on. He would greet me cordially in the corridors or if he came across me reading in the library. If he noticed my awkwardness he didn't comment on it. If I asked for updates on the negotiations, I received a brisk, preoccupied, "No news yet," or "Seems like they're taking their time," as he scanned his phone or disappeared into an office. When I asked Aliyah what was keeping him so distant, she could offer little insight. "I know he's anxious to get the sale out of the way; he's been laying plans for what comes next for a long time," she remarked. Other than that, I barely saw him.

One afternoon I heard a commotion on the large balcony, a strange percussive sound interspersed between brief grunts and shouts. When I went to investigate, I discovered Aliyah completely absorbed in the practice of some kind of martial art. Using a long bamboo stick, I watched her silently as she twirled expertly and effortlessly around a large, suspended piñata-like pigskin bag. The blows seemed vicious although she exercised them with the minimum of effort in graceful, deliberate moves, almost like choreographed dancing. The muscles in her arms betrayed a slight sheen of perspiration but otherwise her body seemed perfectly calm and controlled. She looked up when she saw me.

"I didn't want to disturb you," I said.

"I'm just out of practice."

"Practice for what?"

She stopped and came over to me. "For when I need it," she grinned.

"Here!" and she threw the pole at me. I fumbled the catch and immediately dropped it.

"I'm not the most coordinated person as you can see."

"Perhaps you think about it too much."

I gingerly picked up the pole. It felt lighter in my hand than I would have thought, but its length made it tricky to balance. She walked behind me and reached around my shoulders to position the pole in my hands. "First find your balance, and then find *its* balance," she said softly. "Take your time, Brea, you're not going anywhere."

I moved my hands around the smooth pole and promptly dropped it again.

"You're thinking," she admonished. "Let your body show you."

I tried again and this time tried to clear my mind. Closing my eyes, I felt the weight of the pole in my hands and gradually sensed it lighten, almost as if it was an extension of my body. Aliyah seemed to sense the shift in my body.

"Good," she encouraged, "Now try a strike."

I hefted the pole and swung. The tip of the pole just grazed past Aliyah's head and she ducked easily.

"The bag preferably, Brea!"

I tried again and this time the pole swished past us both, making an agreeable thud as it struck the bag lightly.

"That's good. Accuracy really isn't bad, just need to work on your strength."

I swung the pole again, this time planting a heavier thud into the bag.

"Keep that up, you'll be expert in no time."

"I doubt that. What is this anyway?"

She picked up another pole. "We call it *Pencak Silat*. It's like kendo although much more physical, the purpose is to use less energy, more poise," she explained. "Martial arts are usually all about control and perfection, or maybe they're part of some kind of spiritual exercise. This is about only one thing—killing your enemy. I think it's probably the deadliest of all martial arts. Here, strike my *toya*."

I repeated the action, but she expertly moved her pole and the strike went through the air missing her entirely. For a while I lost my bearings, then realized she had moved almost behind me, a blind spot to my right.

"Again."

I tried to predict her move and this time the pole hit squarely with hers. I saw her face break into a broad smile. "Girl, you've got this!" she laughed, raising her hand in a high five. As my hand met hers, she used my own stick to push me back, and took a strike of her own on my knuckles. The force of the blow sent my pole reeling out of my hands.

"What the ...!" I breathed, feeling the anger rise inside of me.

"Pick it up!" Beneath her mirth there was that steely edge to her voice again. "Pick. It. Up, Brea." Now she was annoying me, but I tried to keep my anger under control as I slowly lifted the stick out of her reach and stood up straight.

"It's never over. Ever. Unless you say it's over, Brea. Don't walk away; don't relax until you're sure you're safe. Always, always try to remember that."

"Okay." Trying to immediately catch her off guard, I struck a blow, landing in the middle of her stick and catching her off guard. She easily regained balance but then feigning a blow to her left, I jabbed to her right and my stick hit her right thigh, probably landing with more force than I intended.

"Remember, fight with your head, Brea, not your heart—but that was good." Just at that moment I heard someone clapping behind me.

"I think I've arrived just in time to save you," Jai Khan laughed at Aliyah. For some stupid reason I felt embarrassed that he'd seen my clumsy performance. But there was a glint in his eyes as he said, "May I speak with your pupil before she actually kills you?"

I gladly surrendered the pole to Aliyah and followed him into the house.

"Aliyah's making a fighter of you? I'm glad; we could use the help," he said.

"Even she's not that good of an instructor." I wasn't sure why I felt so self-conscious around him, but his effect on me was beginning to become more noticeable, like some ridiculous Victorian romance. Playing Cathy to his Heathcliffe wasn't a role that sat well with me; it wasn't a familiar feeling and I really wasn't sure I liked it. He led me into the interior of the compound through a maze of corridors to what I assumed was his office.

"So, this is the nerve center?" I asked. "Where it all happens?"

"Today it is," he grinned, "but I much prefer to be a moving target."

"I can't imagine why."

"The good fortune of operating many different companies from different locations affords me the opportunity to be ... effective wherever I am, the offices in Dhaka where we first met, for example, being just one of them."

"And here?"

"Here is different. This place is a little more important to me."

"The library is impressive."

"Thank you. I first came here as a boy. My father was in politics and he was invited here as part of a trade delegation. Later, when the opportunity came for me to be able to purchase it I didn't hesitate. It's been quite the hole-in-the-wall for us, a useful occasional refuge, ever since."

"And you followed your father into the family business? I didn't think a man like you would have much time for politics."

He smiled. "What was it Pericles said. 'Just because you don't take an interest in politics doesn't mean politics won't take an interest in you?' In my experience, Miss James, just staying alive is political."

"That seems to be a popular view around here."

He offered me a seat on a comfortable arrangement of couches and I noticed immediately that this room was remarkable from the rest of the compound as it seemed to have some personal touches to it. Behind a desk, a photograph hung showing Khan in full flying suit next to what looked like a military aircraft. An antique looking rifle was mounted above, and next to it a photograph of an older man and I wondered if it might be his father. Incongruously, a Yankees baseball hat was thrown on one of the chairs.

"You've been to America?"

"Several times, yes," he followed my gaze, "Although I'm actually more of a Mets fan." There, bizarrely, we actually had one thing in common.

"You do … business there?" I asked carefully.

"I have a cousin who owns several restaurants in New York."

"Like shawarma places?"

"Burger King, actually," he smiled.

He fell silent and after I moment I asked, "What was it you wanted to speak to me about?"

"Oh yes, I was just curious about your clients, what you might be able to tell me about them?"

"I think that's confidential information between me and the client I represent."

"I'm not sure you represent anyone at the moment unfortunately, Miss James," he said gently. "But Bowden and Lowe—what did you say to me on our first meeting? I'm naturally interested in people who are interested in what interests me? I was merely wondering whether you knew them or had perhaps conducted business with them before?"

"Not well. There are many boutique brokers who specialize in particular periods or types of art. They seemed to specialize, or at least be especially interested, in Middle and Far Eastern antiquities."

"You've met in person?"

"No, phone conferences mostly. They're in the suburbs outside Washington—somewhere north of Arlington, somewhere I seem to remember. Why?"

"Washington?"

"Well, yes, I guess. Why?"

"No special reason. Did they offer you any assistance when you arrived in Bangladesh? Additional security, an escort perhaps?"

"No, but I didn't ask either. Before you came along, I really wasn't aware that I needed one," I tried to add pointedly.

"But you mentioned you'd been contacted by some branch of law enforcement?"

"I think you know that."

He smiled again. "Quite possibly I do, but I'm as eager to conclude this transaction as you yourself are, Miss James, and I just want to know who I'm dealing with."

"Well, I think you were the one who changed the rules, Mr. Khan."

He looked at me. "I wonder if that's really true?" And then as if interrupting his own train of thought he suddenly asked, "Who is the insured for the Goddess?"

"There is no insured for the Goddess. Like many antiquities it's generally accepted to be priceless—literally beyond price, beyond replacement. Even more so in the Goddess's case as it's never been sold at auction. I can't think of any underwriter who would be willing to take on that kind of risk. It's literally incalculable"

"It's not insured at all?"

I shook my head, now curious where this was going.

"Does it not strike you as a little odd then that they would send a well-respected and, I'm sure, expensive agent such as yourself to ensure its return?"

I shook my head. "Although the Goddess cannot be insured, the transaction certainly is. It makes perfect sense to me that they'd want an experienced negotiator to ensure the deal is successfully completed."

"They?"

"Whoever my client, Bowden and Lowe are representing."

"And that would be ... ?"

I smiled at this. He was definitely fishing. "I don't know, and anyway I wouldn't be at liberty to tell you if I did. I'm assuming a historical society or museum with deep pockets. It's likely that nothing very much will be done with the figurine for a while, legitimacy is key to any institution caring about its reputation, particularly if it's publicly funded. Once it's established that the Goddess has been legitimately sold, and some kind of paper trail can be found to verify that, it could then be offered at auction."

He nodded and was quiet for a while. Outside, the jungle was hushed in the midday heat and despite the breezes playing from up the valley, it was warm and silent in his office. I felt the same odd tension I had experienced dining with him on my first night here.

Suddenly he said, "Aliyah is looking after you?"

"If anything, she's over attentive, but then I think that's the job you've given her, right?"

"If I said it was for your own safety, I doubt you'd believe me. Is there anything I can provide for you to make your stay more comfortable?"

"No, no I just need to get back to my life."

"Naturally. Well, I'm sorry to keep you from your practice."

"Believe me, I was glad of the interruption. You seem to be making a habit of rescuing me."

He gave me a questioning look.

"Aliyah told me about the rewards offered to the *mastaans*. I didn't know, and I wanted to thank you. I still don't agree with your methods but I realize that I've probably been ... ungrateful."

He waved away my embarrassed half apology. "I can be clumsy at times, particularly when it comes to ... well, let's just say it was good business," he smiled awkwardly. "Perhaps my interests here intersect with those of your client. I, too, need the services of an accomplished negotiator, and right here I have the best."

"Begrudgingly, right here," I echoed.

"I wish it were otherwise, Miss James, believe me." His eyes fell on me for longer than I felt either of us were comfortable with. He coughed and shuffled some papers on his desk and I sensed the audience was over. As I stood to leave, I noticed him glance to my hands where, to my surprise, blood had formed over my bruised knuckles.

"You should get Aliyah to look at that, even the smallest wound can get infected easily here, and we can't have any harm coming to you, can we, Miss James?"

The next few days went by in a blur. In spite of everyone's assurances, it was only now that I actually believed that I wasn't going to be harmed. Freed from the shadow of that, I took full advantage of my enforced vacation. I swam in the beautiful, natural aquamarine water of the pool, slept in the afternoons and ate a succession of beautifully prepared meals, sometimes alone, sometimes with Aliyah introducing me to new and astonishing Asian flavors. I found one of the staff who tested my strategic thinking over games of chess on the kitchen's commis table and where language was no barrier, and some mornings I joined Aliyah with her morning yoga routine, together stretching to greet the sunrise as it filtered into the valley. During this time I saw little of Jai Khan himself. Occasionally I might surprise myself and come across his office on my daily explorations of the compound. He would either be on the phone, lost in conversation or the door would be shut. I somehow felt I wanted to be with him, to help with whatever negotiations he had entered into to secure the Goddess. I missed talking with him and felt strangely that I wanted to learn more about him, more about his self-imposed mission. Aliyah, on the other hand, seemed omnipresent; leaving me on my own to read or rest, she seemed to appear ninja-style from nowhere whenever I needed something. She was true to her word, keeping me close at all times. Some nights during my brief stay at the compound, she even came to my bed.

"May I sit?"

The absurdity of him asking permission in his own home made me smile. I was reading in the library, lost in the cool stacks of books and comfortable sofas, and his sudden presence took me off guard.

"I feel I'm interrupting you," he said.

"Did you know the Chinese wrote five volumes just on breathing?" I said, not looking up from the book I'd been absorbed in all afternoon.

"You've been acquainting yourself with the Dao?"

I nodded. "Among other things, yes."

He smiled, "Always looking for answers, Miss James?"

I let that hang and instead closed the book and looked up at him.

"I wanted to tell you that I'm leaving. So, too, you'll be relieved to hear, will you be."

"So, the Goddess ... ?"

"Yes," he nodded, "the Goddess. The other party has agreed to my terms and, other than just some formalities to conclude, we can have you home with the Goddess within days. I hope I've proved to be true to my word, Miss James, and when you travel back I will personally guarantee your safety."

"I appreciate that, thank you."

"Not at all. I know I brought here against your will, but you've been a welcome guest and now you're leaving us. I appreciate you're too much of an astonishing woman for any harm to come to you."

"Astonishing? Now you're flattering me, I think."

"Not at all. *Summa cum laude* at Sarah Lawrence, a doctorate in International and Public Affairs from the Watson Institute at Georgetown. Captain of the Ladies First Eleven. I think all that's pretty astonishing, should I go on?"

"Oh please," I said. "I'm just loving this."

"You joined Conner, Brigham and Snow, quickly becoming their youngest partner after which you quit to start your own company. You've never married, live well but modestly and, it appears, date infrequently, usually with, in my opinion, seemingly wildly inappropriate partners."

"Wow, you really did check up on me," I laughed. "All of that was a little bit more than I remember putting on *my* Instagram." I put the book down and stood up, level with his face.

"As I said, I have people."

"Well, thank you. I realize now this could have all gone very differently."

He even slightly bowed, "Of course, it's been my pleasure. In other circumstances I would wish you to come back and visit us but I'm sure you'll be glad to never see this place, or us, again."

"That's not entirely true," I mumbled.

He nodded absently, "Well then, I must leave tomorrow morning ... " He moved to leave, and I had that same feeling I had experienced when we dined together my first night at the compound. I felt immediately lonely, empty—desolate even.

"And what about you? Where will you go after this?" I blurted out, with less control than I would have liked.

He seemed surprised at the question. "Me? Well, the first priority is to conclude the deal and see you home with the Goddess. At some point, I'll return to what you in the West might call the

Border Provinces. The proceeds from our arrangement will help greatly in our struggle.

"That's your home?"

"What passes for home, for now, yes. I should be packing to go." He gave me one of those long looks that always made me think he had something unsaid on his mind,

"I am glad it was you," he said eventually in no more than a whisper.

"Excuse me?"

"I am glad you were sent to finalize the sale of the Goddess. The doubtful advantage of being without any sense of nationalism is that I was perfectly content to sell to any number of buyers—the Russians, the Chinese. I'm glad it was you."

"And why is that, Mr. Khan?"

"Because I think I might have very much regretted never having the opportunity of meeting you." He smiled awkwardly and then added, "Now, I should really leave you alone and back to enjoying Lao-Tzu."

"What if I don't want to be alone?" I said to his back, in a whisper that matched his.

He turned, "I'm not sure I quite understand you," he said hesitantly.

I stood there for a moment, suddenly aware of the simple sarong I was wearing, and that the soft batik would be barely concealing my body to him. In that instant I felt an overwhelming sense of calm, and I could only think about how I suddenly wanted to be with him, aware of my own heartbeat, of the warmth of my skin, and how much I wanted to touch him, to be held by him. And even as I thought it, I instantly dismissed the stupid idea. The thought of me and some tribal gangster having any kind of connection was plainly stupid.

He looked at me carefully with, I felt, the practiced eyes of a man who had probably loved many women before. There seemed to be something conflicted about him, as if hesitating, then he walked towards me and held me gently in his arms. I felt my body instantly relax in his embrace with the realization it was too late now for second guesses then suddenly winced as he touched the spot where I had been so recently tranquillized.

"I promise I will never drug you again," he apologized, as we both laughed and the awkward tension left the air.

"And they say romance is dead," I sighed.

And then he pulled my face to his eyes, searching mine as if asking permission.

"Yes," I simply whispered, and he kissed me. I had never really believed the part in every romance novel when the heroine receives a kiss that makes her realize everything she's been missing, from every kiss, from every other man she'd ever experienced. It seemed just like a frivolous construct, but at that moment I understood exactly what that felt like. It was the slowest, yet most passionate kiss I'd ever received, as if he had been saving everything up, denied until given permission to do so. He held my face so gently but his tongue danced hungrily in my mouth, his hands moving freely over my body, awakening all kinds of sensations anywhere he touched me. In contrast to the moment before, everything now felt perfect, natural, the way it was meant to be. Taking his outstretched hand, he led me down a short corridor and into a room I hadn't seen before, his bedroom.

The room felt cool, darker than the library and it gave me confidence. Standing in his bedroom, I untied and stepped out of the sarong, barefoot, naked.

"This might ... complicate things" he whispered.

"It's already complicated."

"But you know I have to leave tomorrow."

"There is still tonight. There's still now, and I want you," I whispered in a voice that I didn't even recognize as my own. "Please." He began showering me with kisses, on my lips, on my neck in a jumble of kisses and frantic caresses, his hands strong and firm on my body. I undid his shirt and as I pulled it from his shoulders I hesitated, I'm sure I must have even gasped. His bare chest revealed a shocking map of pain and violence, his history written in a mass of livid scars and ancient wounds. Seeing his body like that changed something in me and I felt some kind of mysterious compulsion to not just fuck this man but to somehow learn how to love him too. His kisses had their own narrative too, that with all he had seen, and with a better understanding of what this represented to him, here would be a man who would meet my wild ardor with a more thorough understanding of what my body really needed. He made everything easy and effortless, savoring me unhurriedly, leaving no part of my body untouched. His mouth on my ears, my throat, across my breasts, neglecting nothing. When he traveled down my stomach I practically squealed with the sensation of his breath on my pussy. I spread for him shamelessly and beckoned him up to me, but he lazily continued caressing me with his tongue until my clit felt on fire, until I was begging him to fuck me. He slid into me with that same easy grace. I forget how many times I came that night—it seemed a succession of easy orgasms—like one long roller coaster that I didn't want to end, our bodies moving easily in the night heat of the jungle, the sheen of our sweat capturing the shadows of each other's body in the moonlight. His body moved powerfully above me, now tender and slow, now passionate and wild, his eyes locked onto mine as if he was seeing into my soul.

"My, my, so sleepy! What could you two have been doing all night?" Aliyah said in her usual lyrical way, busily raising the shades and looking at me, amused.

Jai had gone; the staff were also dispatched, she informed me.

"We're pulling out of here the moment the deal is concluded, so I get to have you all to myself for a few more days," she chortled good-naturedly. "Breakfast by the pool, clothing optional!" She flung a silk *pareo* at me and left me to fully awaken.

Aliyah had been correct; the compound felt deserted. Walking to the pool, the corridors felt silent and empty. I found her pouring from a pitcher of apricot juice, patting the seat next to her.

"I've been instructed to tell you that we're flying to Lahore in two days' time," she announced. "You'll be given the Goddess there, and from there we'll get you back home to the States."

"And the money?" I asked.

"Jai Khan is having it transferred from your clients at Bowden and Lowe tomorrow. It's done, congratulations!"

"I'm not sure I had anything to do with it at all."

"But you'll return with the statue, and you'll be able to collect your finder's fee."

"And you're not concerned I'll tell my story to the press, alert the authorities about everything I've witnessed here?" I teased.

She laughed. "That you've been detained in a luxury private home while a business deal was finalized to obtain a priceless artifact for a fair market value? Forgive me, Brea, if I'm failing to see the charges!"

"Well, to start with I've been drugged, imprisoned and assaulted by two people!" I protested.

"Seduced, not assaulted—I certainly didn't hear much objection, and two ... two people?" She laughed in mock admonishment, "It sounds like you've certainly been making yourself at home!"

Life could have continued in this strangely lovely prison for days while Jai and, thousands of miles away, my clients Bowden and Lowe negotiated my fate. I felt helpless, resigned, but I suppose most of all, relieved. Now that we were preparing to leave—and I would finally be going home—I realized there was a part of me, a big part of me, that felt uneasy and strangely divided. It wasn't just my memorable night with Jai Khan (something we had both told ourselves would not—could not—ever be repeated) or the unexpected friendship I had enjoyed with Aliyah. There was a sense of purpose that surrounded Jai Khan, a sense that something important was happening here, something that I was both strangely drawn to and wanted to become part of, a feeling of belonging. The more I turned it over in my mind during those last few otherworldly days at the Sanctuary of Clouds, the less sense it made. I told myself this was nothing more than a bizarre, romantic interlude in my life and that the lives of these people were really not my fate, not my fight.

Yet, as it happened, I could have spared myself all this fruitless soul searching because the next day the helicopters came.

4 | BRAHMAPUTRA

Afternoons at the compound had taken on a lazy rhythm. Aliyah and I would spend most of the time together, somehow more urgently now that my time with her seemed to be ending.

Late that afternoon, she asked, "Is she beautiful?"

"Is who beautiful?"

"The Goddess." We were lying in bed. The quiet of the now deserted house was magnified by the heady drowsiness of the afternoon. I was tracing my fingers down her very supple spine, fascinated by the beautifully tattooed adornment of characters in Chinese and Arabic script.

"Well, she's 4,000 years old, so if older women are your thing … and time hasn't been kind. She's also very petite, about forty centimeters I've been told and, oh, she has no arms," I murmured.

"No arms? That's terrible!" she protested.

I kissed a Chinese figure on the middle of her back, loving how accustomed her body had now become to me, how the taste of her had become so familiar to me, exuding something clean but exotic and spicy.

"The Bactrian craftsmen had a thing about female form, "I whispered, "and limbs seemed to get in the way of the curves."

"Well, I agree with highlighting the curves part," she said lasciviously, rolling over and sliding her hands from my hips to my lower belly, kissing my hair and face.

"And was she a Goddess?" she whispered, her deep brown eyes locked into mine.

"Or a princess, but more likely a deity who was worshiped."

"Worshipped?" she nodded slightly and slipped beneath me, down my belly to nuzzle between my thighs. "Like this perhaps?"

"Mmmm, revered, yes ... her people likely adored her."

"Adorable," Aliyah purred.

I felt her suddenly tense, lifting her head from between my legs.

"Wha ... ?"

"Shhh, listen!"

It took a moment or two, but I could hear it too. A distant faint buzzing, causing the air itself to vibrate.

"My rescue party!" I exclaimed to no one in particular, and leapt up to run out to the veranda.

At first, they weren't easy to see against the deep golden glow of the setting sun, but as my eyes adjusted to the glare, three large, black helicopter gunships swung up the valley, their beetle-like fuselages glinting off of the sun, heading immediately toward the compound. Moving with a speed that only she was capable of, Aliyah suddenly appeared at my side, grabbed my arm and jerked me back inside the house.

"Get down, stupid!"

The helicopters continued up the valley, low against the tree line, and stopped short of the compound, hanging almost motionless, buzzing like angry dragonflies. All around them the jungle suddenly fell eerily silent.

"Brea, run. Just run!" Aliyah shouted at me.

Almost immediately there was the sound of glass smashing, a roaring heat fueled by a succession of loud explosions. Grabbing clothes and shoes I chased Aliyah out of the bedroom and down the long internal corridor practically skidding into the staff area and the kitchens. Above me, I heard bullets clatter through the roofing, perhaps where we had lain just moments before. As we ran through the kitchen, bullets whistled through the walls, bouncing off the kitchen counters and the pots and pans, shattering china into shards, with glass, debris, dust and smoke showering on us. At the end of the kitchen, Aliyah pulled open a small, almost concealed door, and we both practically fell down a long flight of stone steps. The noise above us swelled to a deafening intensity, as more explosions shook the ground around us. At the bottom of the steps, the ground sloped off along a long dark corridor, a tunnel lined in ancient brickwork, permeated with tree roots and musty with the smell of vegetation and soil. The sounds above us seemed more muffled now, but Aliyah didn't slow her pace, running through the dark for what seemed like a good half mile until we came to a heavy steel door. To one side there was a storage closet, and with the aid of a flashlight, Aliyah began quickly rummaging through the contents, pulling out a military style rucksack. Despite the commotion and endless detonations above us, I was amazed that she calmly selected and packed a number of items so coolly, unhurriedly yet fiercely concentrating, while I barely got my breath back and stepped into the bundle of clothes I was carrying.

"What's happening?" I gasped.

To my amazement, she pulled an assault rifle from the closet and with a practiced familiarity, shoved in a large magazine of bullets arming the high-powered weapon.

"Do you still think they were your rescue party, Brea?" she said. I didn't like the sound of her voice now, dead and devoid of all the softness of before. She sounded like a warrior.

She must have seen my face fall.

"Listen, they probably didn't know you were even here," she said only slightly more gently. "You would have been nothing more than collateral damage, but if you were the target then we have bigger problems than I thought—*you* have bigger problems that I thought."

The tunnel was quickly filling with thick acrid smoke, and Aliyah cast a glance back up the way we had come. She quickly finished dressing and slung the rucksack over one shoulder, the assault rifle in her other hand.

"Shall we go?"

"Go? Go where?" I said.

"Out of here." She checked something on her phone quickly, before expertly taking it apart and wrecking it, scattering the various components and grinding them underfoot. "This way." She pushed on the heavy door, opening a rush of fresh air after the dank and now smoke-filled tunnel, opening it out into thick jungle vegetation.

"Now run. Brea!"

Coughing and blinded by the smoke, for a moment it felt good to be in the fresher air until I risked a look back and, not far away, I saw the helicopters lingering watchfully, their searchlights piecing the inky blackness as they ghoulishly surveyed their work.

We ran and jogged all night along a trail I could neither see nor determine, but which Aliyah navigated confidently. If ever we felt assurance that we'd maybe put enough distance between us and the destroyed house, the rumble of helicopters and probing search-lights kept us moving until at last they seemed in the far distance. Cursing that I'd given up my morning runs, and all the other many fitness regimes I'd started since leaving college, I struggled not to lose Aliyah in the darkness. I had taken to wearing just a simple sarong tied loosely around my hips, particularly after the staff had left, but today at least I had worn shoes, although these were not for hiking. Aliyah had the easy, measured run of an athlete, and perpetually watching the trail ahead she seemed to move with an effortless speed and at the same time seemingly without sound. When I begged her to rest, she'd slow and we'd walk until I felt I could pick up the pace again. At one point we briefly stopped for water from Aliyah's essential rucksack, and she quickly sprayed my body and hers with some kind of insect repellent.

"Will this help with the spiders?" I gasped.

"What spiders?"

"You know, the neurotoxin ones?"

"Sure it will, Brea," she grinned, "although, okay, I may have exaggerated that threat a little to get you to stay."

I was too tired to be mad at her, and anyway after that, the ceaseless biting from a thousand different bugs didn't seem so noticeable and I only needed to worry about the pain in my legs. Aliyah may have overstated the threat of the jungle to me previously, but as we ran on and the night became thick with the hoots, growls and screams of nameless animals and birds, my nerves were shattered on that grueling hike, aware that probably a thousand pairs of eyes watched us belonging to who knows what.

At some time I gauged to be near dawn, I just stumbled and fell exhausted. I knew my feet were blistered and in bad shape, my lungs felt they were burning and the strength in my legs seemed to have finally evaporated.

Several feet ahead of me Aliyah came back, resting her hands on her thighs for a moment. "It's okay, rest up a minute. We're very nearly there," she whispered, "but I need to go on ahead and check the coast is clear."

"You're not going to leave me?" I said, realizing immediately how lame that sounded.

She looked at me carefully, as if trying to determine something, then said, "Have you ever used a gun?" I shook my head and she pulled another weapon from the bag; this time a handgun.

"This is a Glock 17," she explained. "It's accurate and easy to use and it also has only a slight kick." She showed me how to arm and aim it, and again I was amazed how such a graceful woman could be so expert in the handling of firearms. It made me wonder again about what Jai had revealed of her background and who she really was.

"I'm not sure ..." I mumbled. "I mean, I don't think I can use it."

She looked at me fully to meet my eyes. "When the time comes—if the time ever comes—you'll know what to do, Brea, believe me." She pushed the pistol into my hands and closed my fingers around the cold hard metal.

"I shouldn't be gone long, just please don't shoot me when I come back," she smiled reassuringly. She hugged my shoulders briefly and then with a half wave disappeared into the gathering mist and darkness of the jungle.

Dawn was breaking, but it was taking its time, and along with it, a muted chorus of new jungle sounds began to echo around the trees. It seemed odd to me that the cacophony of the waking jungle that I had found so comforting at the compound now seemed like taunts, and my rising sensation of fear was only amplified by the symphony of bird songs and alarming cries of what I hoped were monkeys. Wraiths of mist clung to the jungle canopy, giving the forest an eerie, otherworldly quality, and I clutched the cold steel of the Glock closer, even though I really had no confidence in using it. I felt tired and lonely and desperate and I couldn't even begin to recount everything that had happened to me since I stepped off the plane in Dhaka. I had no phone, no way of communicating, and was sitting alone in a jungle somewhere with a gun I was more frightened of than the noises around me. I was totally lost in the hopelessness of my thoughts when I felt something touch my shoulder.

With her almost supernatural stealth, I had never even sensed Aliyah coming back. The shock of her touch sent me into her arms, crying hysterically.

"Woah, it's okay! *You're* okay, Brea, it's really not far now. We're going to make it," she said reassuringly.

She carefully relieved me of the Glock, and taking my hand, she pulled me onto my feet and made me follow her, tracking another barely traceable forest trail. Here, the path immediately descended, gradually at first and then more steeply. Soon we were having to cling onto the thick overhanging vines to keep from sliding down into steep, slippery valleys. After an hour, I could hear the sound of rushing water, and a short while after, we were carefully sliding down a steep mud bank into a dense undergrowth of mangroves. Beyond it, I could make out a rushing torrent that I understood must be the Brahmaputra. Aliyah's description had been right, the river looked menacingly deep, wide and fast flowing and, in the weak breaking light of dawn, wildly dangerous.

"I'm not sure I can swim across, Aliyah," I said nervously.

"I'm really hoping we don't have to," she whispered back and, disappearing further into the undergrowth, she began frantically pulling at the vegetation. At first I was alarmed, thinking my always in control protector had finally lost it, until I saw that along with the vines and roots she was soon uncovering a camouflaged tarpaulin, and it was only then that I realized that the very ground we were standing on was some kind of structure. As we worked together on clearing the brush, the sleek surface of a boat became visible beneath. It was well hidden under the tangle of vegetation and branches and after working for some time we eventually freed it. The craft was an impressive, powerful looking launch, and as Aliyah quickly made it ready and prepared the engines, I stowed the tarpaulin and untied it from its remaining mooring cables before joining her in the cockpit.

"This is where we hope," she muttered, and turned the ignition. The engine weakly stuttered then failed. The jungle around us seemed suddenly strangely silent, as if the business of greeting a new day was put expectantly on hold by our uninvited intrusion. I saw a frown briefly cross Aliyah's face as she turned the ignition again, cursing softly under her breath, but on the third try it exploded into life, shattering the pregnant silence. Her concern changed to a wide grin and without any preamble, she expertly engaged the boat and we smoothly moved out onto the open river. Only when

74

she was sure we were free of the last remnants of our camouflaged foliage, Aliyah opened up the three powerful Yamaha engines and we roared downstream.

For the first few miles of the river, I don't think either of us were capable of speech, both of us trying to make sense of everything that had happened in the night.

"Are we ... safe?" I ventured, eventually as I stretched out my legs and began messaging my feet.

"*Safer*," she acknowledged carefully, "but we're also really exposed here on the river so everything's relative until I can get you on a plane home. Why don't you check out below and see if you can find some food?" The boat seemed to be exceptionally well equipped for an emergency escape, the lockers full of every kind of weaponry and provision. Along with a basic galley kitchen, there was also a stash of food and medical supplies. Someone had clearly laid elaborate plans in the event of what had just happened happening, and I wasn't sure if this level of elaborate planning was Aliyah's own survival initiative or a reflection of the scope of the Khan organization. I came up on deck with two mugs of instant coffee and a packet of stale crackers.

"Maybe you can imagine it's Javanese," I ventured.

She took a gulp, not taking her eyes off the river ahead or the surrounding jungle around us, and then touched her mug to mine. "Best coffee I've ever tasted."

As the sun came up and gained strength, the mist evaporated and the river widened, providing a glass-like surface downstream. I know we both felt the same relief about escaping from the destruction of last night's raid, and no matter how exposed we were, as the morning wore on, the river seemed to dispel some of the nightmarish memories of our night in the jungle. At one point Aliyah glanced over to me, concern written on her brow and reached to hold my face.

"Hey, you okay?' she said, risking a smile.

"I'm fine. I'm just sorry about last night," I said. "I really just lost it."

"Nah, you did just fine, girl, really, this wasn't part of the deal. And if it's any consolation, I did not see that coming at all," she grumbled into the wind. In the soft light of the morning, she seemed somehow even more beautiful, even more in her element with her thick hair fan fanned by the breeze, her skin glowing, from either last night's exertions or the sparkling light from the river.

"I don't know how you and Jai can live like this—always hunted, always looking over your shoulder. I mean, how can you stand it?" I asked.

She thought for a moment, her eyes watchfully scanning the river. "The way you feel right now? That incredible feeling of exhaustion but at the same time there's some kind of weird elation—that everything seems amplified ... that?"

"Yes," I nodded, "that's exactly how it feels."

"That's what you want. That's the feeling that keeps you alive. *Suaka Awan* was the most secret of Jai's properties—and I mean *way* secret, yet they obviously found it. That's unusual. Something's just way off." She fell silent for a moment, and I imagined she was probably turning a dozen different scenarios over in her mind.

"Is what happened something to do with me?" I asked.

She took her eyes off the river to look at me for a long moment, as if she was wrestling with exactly that same thought.

"Honestly, Brea, I don't know. I'm not sure why, but like I said, something's really off."

"Do you think Jai's okay?"

"I'm not sure if Jai is even alive," she said softly, her eyes turning back to the river ahead. "You know, we've always had an understanding we'd die for each other—and I really believe that—but we both know the world we live in, and life can be cheap sometimes. Many of our friends, our family, have been killed, and even though you do everything to prevent it, the saddest part is that you start to get used to it in the end."

Even as she said it, I didn't think for a minute she actually believed that. But I wasn't sure what to believe myself. Less skilled than Aliyah in being able to compartmentalize my thoughts and act rationally, I was just a jumble of emotions after that terrifying and sleepless night. The hedonistic tranquility of being held captive in *Suaka Awan* had lulled me into an obviously false sense of security. I'd wasted time as a guest of Jai Khan and suddenly released, I had no idea what came next. When I had arrived in Dhaka, I was only concerned with completing one simple transaction, working at something that had become so familiar to me it almost seemed second nature. Now, and within such a short space of time, I had become more inextricably caught up in the lives of Aliyah, Jai, and the complexities of the Goddess than I could have possibly imaged. I had no idea how I felt about them now and how it all related to my life, my *real* life, in New York. The things I'd always felt so certain about now seemed inaccessible and distant, belonging to another world. Another life.

Calmed by the steady thrum of the boat engines, I felt increasingly drowsy and must have slept until I was snapped awake by a change in the boat's vibrations. It was already late afternoon and Aliyah had slowed the boat, carefully navigating any bends in the river that could conceal danger or discovery. Once she saw I was awake, she instructed me to take the wheel, and disappeared below decks briefly, coming back with a deep blue *jabhala.*

"From here on in, you look at no one, you talk to no one. You make yourself as invisible as possible," she instructed, as she wrapped the scarf around me, tucking in my hair and covering my neck and shoulders. I nodded without comprehending what might come next, but a few miles further down the river we pulled up against a low riverbank and Aliyah quickly moored and concealed the boat under the camouflage tarpaulin and helped me onto land. It felt like we were in the middle of nowhere, the jungle having now given way to flat farmland with only the beginnings of a few scattered signs of human cultivation. But Aliyah had retrieved a GPS device from the boat and confidently led the way and after just a short hike, we came to the outskirts of a small, rural village. In the drowsy heat of midafternoon, the place seemed quiet and deserted except for some chickens scratching in the dust and a dog sleepily sheltering in the shade of a jackfruit tree. Behind a dilapidated outhouse, Brea led us straight to an equally dilapidated Isuzu pickup. Boldly retrieving a concealed ignition key under the dashboard, she told me to get in, and we simply drove calmly out of the village.

"Is this just another day at the office for you?" I asked incredulously.

"It's never that, Brea. Never ever. But sometimes it helps to have a contingency," she almost smiled. "When you establish a safe-house, the first thing you do is make sure you have plenty of ways out of it."

The road was barely passable, and we endured several miles of bumpy, almost impassable jungle track before finally coming to a paved road and then, a few miles further on, a major freeway. By nightfall, we were in the city, the lights, the noise, the mass of people all around us dizzying to me after being in the solitary embrace of the jungle. Once in the city, Aliyah quickly abandoned the main roads and squares in favor of a maze of darkly lit side streets and narrow alleyways, carefully avoiding police or the chance of appearing in any traffic cameras. When I was certain we must be lost, Aliyah pulled the truck into a dark, nondescript alley and turned off the engine.

"We're here," she announced, sounding equally as exhausted as I felt.

"Where?" I asked.

"You'll see."

We got out, stretching and yawning, and she beckoned me to follow her through the shadowy streets, past all-night coffee shops and markets, past sleeping houses and appalling slums, where the inhabitants slept under cardboard or corrugated iron—or less—until we reached a deserted square in what I guessed to be the commercial district. Aliyah pulled me back into the shadows and, drawing me close, took my face in her hands.

"This is where I have to leave you, Brea," she said.

"Wait, what?" I was suddenly alarmed. "Stay! You can't just leave me!" I knew it wasn't just fear after all we had been through, but something more. I felt an unexplained, rising hysteria. Even as my captor, I had always felt safe with Aliyah. I certainly felt safer with her than anywhere else knowing that now someone, somewhere was trying to kill us. More than anything, I knew I didn't want to leave her.

"You'll be safe now," she said, calming me down.

"Then come with me."

"I'm wanted by enough people that I'd never see daylight again," she said calmly. "But you're right about what you said on the boat. This isn't your world, and it isn't your fight. Something has gone wrong, and badly wrong. I'm not sure who to trust, I'm not sure I can fix it, and most of all, I'm not sure I can even protect you anymore. You need to go home. This is what you wanted all along, to be free. Now go home where you'll be safe while you still can."

My eyes filled with tears and I knew I was uncontrollably shaking my head. Then, thoughtfully she looked fully at me. "If it helps, understand this: I was never your friend, Brea, only your jailer. You asked me once about the absence of guards. If I had to, if you had escaped and then compromised Jai Khan in any way, you have to know I would have killed you myself. If I find out you were in any way responsible for the helicopters last night, I still might."

Whether she sensed I needed it, or because she just wanted to, she suddenly kissed me, deeply and meaningfully.

"Gotta go girl," she whispered.

"But alone ... here in the middle of the city?"

"No, not quite alone, Brea," she said patiently, and pointed across the square.

Following her gaze, and set back from the street, was a large, walled brick colonial-looking building. Even in the darkness, the large brass plate on the embassy gates was well illuminated. She pulled the *jabhala* from my head and fanned out my blond hair.

"Walk slowly towards the gates with your hands up," she said quickly. "They're nervous about suicide bombers here, especially women. I'll be watching, but these are your people, so just don't panic and you'll be okay. Now go!"

I felt her untangle from my arms, the absence of her, of her body, her warmth, her presence making our separateness even more acute, but I remember numbly walking towards the gates, my mind on a million things—Aliyah, the destruction in the jungle, Jai, the danger I was still in. I'd made it halfway across the square when a massive spotlight flicked on, bathing the whole square in the harsh glare of the blinding xenon lamps.

"On your knees!" a voice shouted. "Keep your hands up and get on your knees."

"I'm an American citizen!" I yelled back. I thought for a moment about the irony of surviving capture by one of the biggest crime lords in the region only to be gunned down by my own countrymen. I wondered what it felt like to be shot. Would I feel anything? Would I experience the shock of the hot metal of the bullets slice into my body, or would there just be black nothingness?

"On your damn knees!" The voice yelled more excitedly.

"I'm an American citizen," I repeated as I knelt on the ground. "My name is Brea James. I've just escaped … " Escaped what? I thought about Aliyah's playfulness, the way Jai Khan had made me feel the last night we were together. His beautiful library, now destroyed and in cinders scattered across the jungle floor. "I've just escaped," I whispered into the blinding light, only dimly aware of the tears uncontrollably streaming down my face.

Behind the searchlight's glare I heard the massive gates being dragged open and two marines rushing out. Quickly and unceremoniously they thoroughly frisked me, then grabbing me by both arms, practically carried me inside. As the gates closed behind me, I risked a glance back, but Aliyah had done her ninja thing and had already disappeared soundlessly into the shadows.

5 | NEW YORK

It took me a long time to figure out where I was. I was aware of waking from a lovely, lazy dream and a familiar, luxurious feeling of carnal pleasure—the vivid impression of a talented man between my thighs lazily kissing me there. And then I was awake, back in my apartment in New York and there *was* a man between my thighs, expertly bringing me to orgasm. I yelped and practically leapt off the bed.

"Woah, baby," Scott said. "That was intense!"

"What ... how ... ? I mean, fuck. What's going on?"

"After last night, I thought it would be a nice way to wake up, that's all. I didn't mean to startle you. You seemed into it," he protested. I had to admit, I could feel the betraying wetness between my legs which only served to confuse me more.

"Yes, but ... when did I get back?"

"Back? Back from where, baby?" He was beginning to annoy me.

"Back from Bangladesh," I said slowly.

"I've no idea," he said, now sounding jilted. "You didn't say you were back from anywhere last night."

"Last night?"

"At the conference, we talked about a lot of things, but I didn't know you were just back from anywhere."

"Wait, wait ... just wait a minute." I could feel my voice rising, and with it, some hysteria I was barely managing to control.

"I was in Bangladesh last night."

There was a look on his face that I didn't like, but it looked distinctly as though he thought I was crazy.

"Hey, we drank a *lot* last night, Bree. Sure, maybe ... "

No one calls me Bree, and now I think I was even hyperventilating.

"I believe," I said, as calmly as I could, "I would like you to leave."

He held up his hands warily. "Okay, okay, baby, I'm leaving." Even as I watched him pulling on his pants, I felt a pang of remorse, along with the beginnings of a huge migraine, but I needed time to think, even though I wasn't entirely sure I wanted to be on my own.

"Just want to say ... " he began defensively, "I had a great time last night, if you want to do it again when you're ... you're, you know ... Call me."

His presence had been annoying, confusing me, but now the apartment felt decidedly empty. Worse still, everything felt strange, out of place. *I* felt out of place. I showered, made coffee, took several acetaminophens and tried to clear my mind. I had left New York, when? My ticket stub would be in my bag, but that was lost at the hotel and my phone was who knew where. It was then that I glanced into the kitchen and saw my faithful Birkin Noir in its usual place slung on the counter. This was impossible. I cautiously shifted my gaze to the nightstand where to my disbelief my phone was charging in its usual place. I gingerly lifted it, almost afraid to touch it, the familiar screen now seemingly alien. I hastily checked the date. I had left New York on Monday, and the phone showed Tuesday. But what Tuesday? I had thought it was earlier in the month, but that seemed an age ago. I had left on the third or was it the thirteenth? I was at Jai Khan's retreat for what, a few days? A week maybe? The days had just seemed to run together. Damn this headache and why couldn't I think clearly?

Trying to retrace the memories of the past few days also brought back an aching for Aliyah. Now, that *was* real. I could still feel her body next to me, her lips on mine, but was that last night, or weeks ago? Everything else seemed foggy. I remembered the jungle, I remembered coming through the gates of the embassy, and perhaps an interview with someone—or was it several someones? Then how did I get home, and even back with Scott? I slowed my breathing and tried to calm down. I looked down at my phone again and instinctively called Bowden and Lowe. After several minutes on hold I was put through to a voice I didn't recognize who mysteriously said there were no plans to purchase any antiquities in Bangladesh, and yes they certainly had a record of meeting with me about the Sarianidi Goddess but had subsequently told me they had decided not to pursue the claim. I had no contracts, outstanding fees or expenses with them, but was there anything else they could help with?

And that was only the beginning. When I checked my credit card statements there were no charges related to the trip. Airfare, hotel charges—no trace existed, and when I placed a long-distance call to the Dhaka Imperial saying I needed a copy of my bill, no record could be found of my credit card, or even of my original reservation. My laptop, which I remembered last using on the flight to update some spreadsheets, was in its usual place in my office, plugged in. But when I checked, there was no record of the work I had done on the plane. My calendar showed nothing for yesterday, no notes related to recovering the goddess. My search history showed it was last used yesterday for a recipe I only dimly remember checking days—or was it weeks—ago. Did I dream the whole damn thing? Had Scott put something in my drink and this was some weird hallucinatory date rape hangover? I remembered clearly me inviting him back, seducing him. I remembered the sex. I remembered ... I suddenly had no idea what I remembered. It was as if the whole thing never happened.

In the next few days that feeling of unease became only more intense. Even though it seemed like everything about the past weeks had been expunged, concealed to even the smallest detail, as the following days rolled into weeks there were tiny, reassuring reminders that I wasn't totally losing my mind. Even though all of my clothes and belongings were inexplicably in my apartment—including the Theory shift I had worn on the flight to Dhaka—some things were just imprecisely out of order. My luggage was neatly placed on the floor of my closet instead of above my armoire; my toothbrush was placed on the sink instead of in the bathroom cabinet on its charger; my passport was in my desk drawer instead of in my safe behind the Lovelace O'Neal in the dressing room. There was also the unquestionable proof of a blister on my left foot that I remembered from the all-night trek in the jungle, and the livid bruise on my thumb I had earned learning *Pencak Silat* from Aliyah.

Even so, I was beginning to think Aliyah was right. If everything had happened the way I remembered it, who could I tell? Who wanted to know and what, exactly, would I even tell them? I was held hostage, and had a fleeting one-night stand with the infamous Jai Khan, yet came back without the Goddess, without proof of anything?

The next few weeks my life stubbornly refused to go back to being anything like normal. On the surface everything was as it should be: I picked up cleaning, I shopped for groceries, I even caught up with friends, although in a detached way that I'm sure was obvious. Without the fee from the Bangladesh assignment, I also needed to get back to work and tried to concentrate on a long-delayed fire damage claim. Fortunately, I could work the claim from fire department reports and logs from field agents as I really didn't want to travel anywhere. Even so, New York no longer offered me the familiar comfort it once had. I realized I was just as alone here in my own city as I had been in the jungle. Everything seemed different, not only with me, informed by what I believed I had so recently experienced, but also with the city itself. I smelled the jungle in the garbage nightly piled on the sidewalk; I heard the thrum of the helicopter gunships in the downtown traffic. Most of all, I couldn't keep my mind off Jai. I kept straying back to our brief time together. I missed him; my body ached for him. Were he and Aliyah imprisoned, or even alive? Had whoever sent the helicopters found them in Dhaka and had them killed? I paced the apartment for days wondering what to do; wondering *who* I could talk to; wondering if I was going crazy. Frustratingly, the deeper I dug into just what

87

could have happened to me the past few weeks, the fewer answers I discovered until some weeks later, when I had almost determined to put all of this behind me and reconnect with my life, and I got into an ordinary New York cab and received the biggest shock of all.

It was raining that day, raining in a way that I think it can only rain in Manhattan, and knowing I'd never find a cab in that downpour I had started to make my way to the subway when, with unbelievably good timing, one pulled up alongside me.

"You're being followed," the driver announced as I slid gratefully into the back seat. "Probably to make sure you don't talk to anyone."

He turned, and of all the people I might have imagined driving my yellow cab downtown that day, the last person I could have conjured up would have been Jonathan Byrne.

"Where are we going?" he asked almost conversationally.

"What the fuck!" I replied.

"Well, we can't sit here all day, Miss James."

"My ... hairdresser?" I stuttered, incredulously.

"An address would be helpful."

"Soho—Prince and Lafayette," I managed to say. "Wait—what? Who's following me?"

"Of that I'm not sure, but I have some guesses. Can you direct me?"

"Aren't you supposed to be a cop?" I said, recovering some composure.

"Somehow, I missed my beat duty in New York City."

"Take Broadway," I muttered. He pulled out and, I have to say, with some skill, navigated the crosstown traffic south onto Broadway.

"Are you okay by the way? I hate to say I told you so, but ... "

"No, I'm not even slightly okay ... Wait a minute, you know! You *know* I was there, in Bangladesh!"

"Indeed, I do, although I recall our meeting being quite short, and after our conversation it would seem you disappeared into thin air."

"I was there!" I practically screamed at him, "I didn't just make it all up!"

He looked back at me in his rearview mirror as if I really was a crazy person. "I'm not sure why you would do that, Miss James." Unflappable as ever. "In fact, I would have thought given your recent adventures it would all have been rather unforgettable."

"So how am I even here? Do *you* know how I got home?"

He shook his head. "Now *that* is something of a mystery. We traced you entering the U.S. Embassy in Dhaka, and we've since located you here at your apartment, but no, we don't know how you got home." I almost unconsciously noticed his use of the "we" pronoun again, but this time it seemed less intimidating to me, like parents checking to see you got home okay.

"Curiously, my contacts in the Foreign Office have no trace of you—no record of your flight home, or even entering the country. Nothing," he added.

"So you believe me?"

"Yes, of course I believe you, Miss James."

I found myself babbling, telling him in a rush about the hideout in the jungle and its destruction, and my escape with Aliyah up to arriving at the American embassy in Dhaka. Then I told him about the strangeness of my arrival back in my apartment, the missing time and the erasure of anything connected to the past few weeks.

"Hmmm, that definitely sounds like the CIA," he said casually.

"The C-I-A?" I repeated numbly. After everything that had happened to me in the past few weeks, this was an especially surreal moment. We were speeding down Broadway, passing everything familiar to me—Washington Square Park, Duane Reade, Banana Republic, Starbucks— and yet, Byrne was calmly recounting this fantastical tale that somehow involved me and the CIA?

"You mean, the government?"

"Last time I checked, yes, I believe they are."

"But aren't you the government?

"No," he said slowly. "We're Interpol, and politically neutral. Do you honestly ever listen to me?" he said in mock exasperation.

"So why would the CIA be even slightly interested in me?"

He watched me for a moment in his mirror, then finally said. "I think it's more your latest company they're interested in. In recent years, we … Interpol … have been working very closely with UNESCO, and actually with certain governments around the world, trying to locate some priceless antiquities looted during the Taliban occupation in Afghanistan," he began. "Just like your Goddess, Miss James, we've estimated that some 70,000 objects, many of them priceless, just walked out the door of museums and collections, plundered by Taliban warlords or corrupt custodians— many of whom are still in positions of power." We had stopped at a crosswalk, both of us impassively watching the pedestrians cross, huddled under umbrellas, barking into phones. "We've managed to locate and return over 800 artifacts," he continued, "but many are still unaccounted for—until recently, and the Goddess was one of them."

"Fascinating, but what's it all got to do with me?"

"The Goddess was stolen by a thoroughly unpleasant fellow who was also, unfortunately, the CIA's best hope for helping run the new pro-Western government of the country. You might call it a bribe, but they were anxious to ensure his allegiance to the U.S. so were happy to find a way to reward him for his continued friendship by buying the figurine from him for an outlandish sum. A disguised golden handshake so to speak."

"The CIA were my buyers?"

"Exactly. It's the simplest way of money laundering. Bowden & Lowe, which you've now probably guessed was a front organization, hired you to facilitate a perfectly above-board deal for an anonymous buyer in exchange for a priceless statue, and their guy gets funding for his ... well, political aims—penthouses or luxury yachts or whatever despots spend their money on these days. It's a very sweet little deal. By the way, aren't we nearly there?" he grumbled. "I have to return this cab in twenty minutes."

"Make a right here," I said absently.

"So why go to all the trouble? Why couldn't they just give this guy the money?"

"Oh, I don't know, Miss James. Iran Contra? Supplying aid to the Mujahedeen? Destabilization in the Middle East? Even Vietnam itself—foreign policy gaffes have an unfortunate habit of coming back to haunt you unless you cover your tracks well. Anyway, as it turned out, and unfortunately for all concerned, Jai Khan got in the way, arranged for the artifact to come into his possession, leaving the CIA in the risky position of being potentially exposed for blatantly corrupting a foreign official, which, by the way, is illegal. They were not best pleased. Not pleased at all. They obviously lost their appetite for being altruistic patrons of antiquity, the money exchange didn't happen, and when Khan tried to resuscitate the deal, for good measure they gave his whereabouts to the local authorities, who were only too pleased to send a greeting."

"The CIA wanted to kill me?"

"Of course not, Miss James. But Khan has gotten in the way of an unctuous little deal that had quickly become a potential embarrassment for all concerned. The solution was to ask the Pakistani government to ensure his silence. When balancing the advantages of harboring a known terrorist against the continuation of some substantial American aid, I'm guessing it wasn't a hard decision for them to order up the helicopter gunships. Bit of a shame you were a houseguest at the time. Is this it, by the way?"

We'd arrived at my hairdressers and Byrne pulled over.

"This ... this is just insane," I breathed, exasperated.

"I couldn't agree with you more, Miss James," he said peering at the hairdresser storefront, "and it looks ridiculously expensive, too."

I kicked his seat, and we sat for a moment in silence just idling at the curb. Eventually Byrne said, "By the way, I thought you might like to know that Jai Khan is here. In New York."

I'm not sure how many more surprises I could have taken that day. "What?" I gasped. "He's not dead?"

"No, he's very much alive, and actually we were rather hoping you'd like to meet with him," he said flatly.

"Me? Why? What for?"

"Because he trusts you. And because we're actually rather eager for you to continue the sale."

"Continue the sale? Are you fucking kidding me? I thought you just said they wanted it stopped at all costs!"

"That was then, and although you'll be late for your very important hair appointment if I were to explain the finer points of international geopolitics, let's just say things change, Miss James, and things change quickly. During your escapade in the jungle, CIA Intel were advised that their boy had flown the coop so to speak—some tribal dustup I believe—and as it turns out their new best hope of installing a new pro-Western regime is now none other than your friend Khan. Seems they're now all rather fond of him."

I was thinking of Jai's "same deal different players" speech. How right he was—and how wrong!

A couple huddled next to the taxi and tapped on the window irritably. Byrne casually flicked his "for hire" light off.

"But if he's pro-Western anyway that still doesn't explain why the CIA are so eager to give Khan money, and why are *you* setting this up? I just don't understand any of this bullshit!"

"Calm down, Brea," he said more gently than before. "Just follow the money. Khan is a bad man, a gangster no question, but the reason he stole the Goddess in the first place is because he's desperate to start an uprising, to overthrow the current regime. To achieve that he needs arms—a lot of them. Despite his many sins, arms dealing really isn't his stock-in-trade so to speak, and if he wants them he's going to be forced to get them from an even worst despot and someone the CIA are even more interested in, a rival tribal leader named Siraj Sajjad."

"Yeah, well that's just not true," I protested. "Your info is incorrect if you think he wants in on an arms deal. I know he wants money but it's to build hospitals, infrastructure, schools to improve education ... "

"I don't doubt you *believe* he's a reformer but that doesn't happen without bloodshed, particularly in that part of the world. Even so, it's the likelihood of a deal with Sajjad that makes Khan so interesting. Sajjad is the tribal head of a faction the CIA don't much like—he's a former Al Qaeda commander, responsible for arms deals, human trafficking, heroin, you name it—and now that the CIA's original plan has crashed and burned he could also easily endanger any new peace efforts. However, he's a ghost; no drones, no inside intel, we know literally nothing about him. Helping Khan get on the inside of his organization is probably the only way they'll ever get to reach him. Once they can get Khan interested in money for the deal the trail will lead to Sajjad and once found, he can be, well, neutralized is I believe the term they use. Their brilliant idea is that you resurrect the deal paying Khan for the statue with their money, he'll get his guns to start his revolution of the people, the CIA will get Sajjad and everyone gets to live happily ever after."

Hearing this made my blood boil. I had so believed—so wanted to believe—the story Jai had told me about schools and reform, yet it turned out all along he was only going to spend the profits from the sale of the Goddess on guns.

"Did I lose you?" Byrne asked from the front seat.

"I was just thinking, that's all. You still haven't told me what's in this tidy little deal for you?"

"Ah, quite. Well, Interpol's little bonus from all of this is that a key player in the international heroin and sex trafficking trade is taken out of the game—so that whole nasty business gets a little bit smaller—not to mention a priceless cultural artifact gets lifted out of the criminal black market to enjoy a secure home. Not a bad day's work all around, you might say."

"And while you've all been hatching this mastermind plot, did anyone consider why the fuck should I want to get involved? Did it occur to anyone that I've just been through this nightmare once?"

"Well, apart from helping make the world a much better place—and actually helping your new friend Khan, I'm given to understand it might be in your best interest, Brea. Let's just put it that way."

"In my best interest? You're really gonna have to explain that one to me," I hissed.

He shifted uncomfortably in the driver's seat, and pointedly avoided looking at me in the rearview mirror. "Please try to understand what I'm telling you. As far as the Feds are concerned, you're still something of a loose end. Unwittingly, you've become witness to a highly secret, not to mention illegal, transaction between your government and one, now possibly two, known terrorist groups. That's propelled you to way beyond any tolerable security clearance, and clearly the little charade they put together for your homecoming should be an indication of what they're capable of. Of course, they might be counting on you either losing your mind or forgetting about the whole thing. After all even if you felt compelled to share what you've seen, who is going to believe you? Who would corroborate your story? I'm sure if you behave, you'll have nothing to worry about, but on the other hand, there might be an unexpected tax audit, problems with your credit. I've told you you're already being followed and your government aren't always the nicest people. Oh, and by the way, your new beau, Scott, is one of them. I believe they call it 'intimate surveillance.'"

"That fucker!" I seethed.

"Yes, quite, Miss James. In this business I'm afraid few things are what they seem and, in my experience, very few people are who they say they are."

"And should I apply that same logic to you, too, Mr. Byrne?"

"Well, you've got me there," he grinned, glancing at me in his rearview mirror. "Let's just say some deceits are worse than others."

I let that one go. My head was reeling. This, none of it, made any sense at all. But it was this new revelation about Jai that really shook me. It seemed I had been "sleeping with the enemy" after all. For a moment I watched the rain bead down the window of the cab, quiet but for the occasional swipe of the wipers.

"What makes you think he'll go for it?"

"Khan?" he shifted again uncomfortably in his seat, "Well, I think the prevailing wisdom on that would be that he would be on a need-to-know basis."

"I wouldn't tell him, you mean? I would lie to him?" I threw up my hands in frustration.

"At the moment, Khan believes he's entering into an honest arrangement—a valuable antiquity in exchange for the tools he needs to build a future for his countrymen," Byrne responded calmly. "Our fear—the fear of the CIA, that is—is that if he feels he's being manipulated, if the whole thing is being in a sense *stage managed*, he may seek other suitors, and believe me they are lining up, the Russians, the Chinese ... "

"So please just tell me this, why *would* our government be suddenly so eager to dream up a plan that would put guns in the hands of someone they think is a criminal?"

"I believe that's seen as the beauty of it. As you seem to have gathered, Khan sees himself as something as a Robin Hood with fierce political aspirations and, frankly, if the overthrow of the current regime is his end goal, then the CIA get what they wanted in the first place. They'll have a new friend in the region and, from there, favorable terms for future arms deals, construction and military contracts, etcetera. As you're rapidly finding out, Miss James, the world is neither a simple nor a virtuous place. For goodness sake, we would have probably given him the guns ourselves. It's just neater, and of course, a little less traceable this way."

"Fuck," I said again.

"Exactly," he gave me another one of his cards and told me to get out.

"That's it? That's it? You dump all of this on me and then just leave me here?"

"You'll be late for your appointment."

"Am I supposed to pay you?"

"That would be attempted bribery of a police officer, Miss James, so I'd say no."

Out on the curb, I hesitated, and leaning into his window asked, "And just why should I trust you?"

"That's a good question, and I hate to be blunt, but right now, I'm honestly all you've got. I will be in touch, but please do think about it, Brea—this might be the best solution for your friend Khan too," he shouted, driving away. "Oh, and tell them not to take too much off the bangs, they do look so very fetching on you."

I remember almost nothing about that haircut. I sensed Sebastián flittering around me, but my thoughts weren't even there, completely absorbed by what Byrne had just told me. Piecing together the whole sequence of events that Byrne had just related to me, everything finally made sense, but the story was so unbelievable I could afford to be skeptical. Of all the things he had told me, the revelation that bothered me most was that I had been fucking a spook in my own bed. I idly wondered what Scott had included in his report. *Target made frequent requests throughout the evening that I continue to fuck her harder and made plentiful suggestions in an urgent manner about how this might best be achieved.* I shuddered in sheer embarrassment at the thought. As Jonathan Byrne had pointed out, it seemed I was running out of people to trust. Also, if I was honest, I wasn't that upset about the possibility of seeing Jai again. I just couldn't wait to give the sanctimonious bastard a piece of my mind.

Two days later, in the early evening, I continued my long overdue beauty regime at an unexceptional looking nail salon on the Lower East Side. I took a seat in the waiting room, flicked through a magazine for a few minutes, then rose to use the restroom. The owner indicated the back of the store without looking at me, and I followed a long hallway around a corner to a door which I pushed open into an alley, where Byrne was waiting in a plain sedan car.

"Well done, Miss James" he beamed as he held open the door. "We'll make a spy of you yet."

"I'm just fine with my day job, thanks."

"Please put on the dress, we don't have far to go." In the seat next to me was a long, formal dress in a cleaner's bag.

"Do I want to know why the dress-up in the first place?"

"A fundraiser. Eastern economic growth development. Our guess is that Khan is using it to try and secure a new buyer for the Goddess."

I held up the dress, a perfectly cut bias gown in in a pale lavender. I wondered if Interpol had a style consultant on staff. "Oh, Tom Ford!" I gushed in mock happiness. "You sure know how to impress a girl!"

"I'm sure it's a knockoff, and frankly I would have gone with Givenchy myself, Miss James," he sniffed.

"You didn't choose it just for me?" I pouted.

"I am just an extremely low-level servant of the law, as you know."

"And just how high does the decision making go into what frock the girl is gonna wear to the ball, Johnathan?"

"Let's just say you're quite the *cause célèbre* at the moment, Miss James."

"And do you have instructions as to just what the *cause célèbre* is supposed to wear under this thing?"

"Well, I'm no expert, but I would imagine as little as possible," he murmured wryly.

"Well, no peeking back here," I sighed resignedly, the beautiful dress spread on my lap wondering how on earth it fell to me to play the part of some femme fatale in an all too real-life spy caper.

As I shrugged off my jeans and tee shirt, I quickly realized the gown would be impossible to wear with a bra. Wriggling into the gown in the confined space I further realized I was probably flashing my boobs to anyone watching, bringing back painful memories of high school make-out sessions. Being a perfect gentleman, Byrne kept his eyes on the road but threw a bag into the back containing a purse and a matching pair of heels, unsurprisingly in exactly my size. It was quite the Cinderella moment.

"How come everybody knows *everything* about me?"

"It's the price for being so popular," Byrne quipped, "Speaking of which, there's a microphone and GPS locator sewn into the hem of your dress—we'll be able to hear and know where you are at all times. You'll be quite safe."

"I hear that's quite the couture trend this season. And tell me again what I'm supposed to do?"

"Absolutely nothing. Just be your charming self and have a lovely time. Tell Khan you'd like to resume the deal. He needs the money, so he'll be delighted to see you and you already have a ... relationship, so you'd absolutely be the most logical choice as a go-between."

"And what exactly is the deal I'm offering?"

"Fifty million for the statue, take it or leave it."

"Fifty million!" I wasn't sure I was hearing him correctly. The deal I had brokered with Bowden and Lowe previously was a fraction of that. "That's ridiculous! The Guennol Lioness broke all records when it was sold for fifty-seven million," I protested.

"I regret I'm a little behind in my comparative value of antiquities studies, Miss James."

"The Lioness is a carving, Mesopotamian, some 5,000 years old. Its opening bid at Sotheby's was 8.5 million, but it was sold at nearly 575 million, a record price for any sculpture at auction. I doubt the Goddess would achieve anything close to that."

"Well, let's just say that in this case the amount is more reflective of the need than the value," Byrne acknowledged.

"Meaning, it's exactly the price tag of Jai Khan's small arms deal," I whispered to myself.

We had reached an alleyway behind a massive hotel building. Byrne turned in, slowing the car to stop outside of a loading bay entrance.

"This is it?" I asked. Somehow I had wriggled into the dress without splitting the seams, and hastily finger-combed my hair in Byrne's rearview mirror.

"Yes, through the door, past the kitchens, and beyond that you'll see the ballroom up a flight of stairs. A laptop has been left for you at the concierge desk, and if you can persuade Khan to accept the deal, you'll find the transfer instructions already loaded on it."

Byrne looked uncharacteristically worried. "What aren't you telling me Jonathan?"

He hesitated, looked at me. "Well, um, yes, there is perhaps just one last thing I wanted to mention actually, Miss James."

"Uh oh," I teased.

"You're familiar with the term Stockholm Syndrome, perhaps?" I racked my brains for what little I knew of the Diagnostic and Statistical Manual of Mental Disorders and shook my head.

"No, but please don't tell me it's a virus."

"Not at all. Stockholm Syndrome is the term applied to the connection—possibly expressed even as affection—by a captive for their captor."

"Fascinating, but I need to know this now why?"

"Let's not fool ourselves, Miss James. Khan is undoubtedly a charismatic, some say even charming, man. You're being asked to deceive him, lie to him, possibly put him in danger, and I'm hoping your recent history isn't disposing you to any inclination of affection, or er, attachment." He paused for a second as if waiting for some response. When none came, he continued. "Look, Brea, working undercover requires years of training—conditioning if you like — none of which you've received. When you're as deeply undercover as we're asking you to be, things sometimes, as you've already found out, get a little blurry. It's times like that when you're at your most vulnerable, when your guard is down, when you're wondering if you're doing ... the right thing."

I hesitated for a split-second, wondering if Johnathan noticed. "Affection?" I scoffed. "He drugged me twice, lied to me constantly about who he was and what he stood for, nearly got me killed and left me to die in the jungle. That's probably the most ridiculous thing I think I've heard you say so far."

Byrne looked at me carefully for a long time before saying, "Good, that's what I thought." He opened the door for me and wished me luck.

"You're doing the right thing, Brea," he said after me in his fatherly voice. "Stick with the plan, and you'll be fine."

I followed the maze of hotel kitchens and through the its extensive utility section. After that, the distant sound of a band told me where to go. On the way, I passed a restroom and quickly checked my appearance. Surprisingly, I didn't look too bad for my quick change in the car. In the mirror, however, I realized the dress itself was no more concealing than lingerie, flattering, hugging my waist and skimming over my hips and ass in a way that accentuated my curves. The lavender color certainly complemented my loose, blond hair and despite my nerves, I had to admit that if this didn't attract Jai Khan's attention, nothing would.

I found the fundraiser as Byrne had said, in a large glittering ballroom on the second floor. Matching the lavish decorations, the event had clearly attracted many equally well-dressed guests, but as I entered the room I quickly established there was no sign of Khan. I decided to head to the bar and mix with the other guests as far as that was possible. To be honest I was hardly in the mood for socializing.

Since that cab ride days earlier with Byrne, I had been wrestling with something. Everything was mixed up and nothing quite added up. Most of all, I realized that I resented being used as a pawn and that people I didn't know—powerful people—had deliberately fucked with my private life. I had worked hard on a constructing a deal that was clearly a sham from the very beginning, putting me in the middle of a much bigger plot that, even now, I found I could barely understand. The whole botched cover-up for my trip to Bangladesh was a lie, and the Scott thing still bothered me most of all. I would have loved to have called his number and told him what I thought of his lying ass, but I didn't want to give him the satisfaction. And now Jonathan was asking me to be an integral part of exactly the same kind of deception, in a deal that I had to assume his people had somehow revived with the CIA.

On the surface, it looked as neat as he had explained, with everyone getting what they wanted, but what was nagging at me the most was the fear of repeating the same mistake again. The difference this time would be that it required me to play a role, one that was making me feel more and more uncomfortable. High on that list was the fact that despite their reputations, I was potentially putting people that I had come to trust, and that had even saved my life, in danger. The more I thought through that, the more I knew something deep inside me was secretly hoping Jai wouldn't show. I could tell Byrne I had done my best to be a team player, but now everyone just had to leave me alone. While the other guests would smile and nod at me, I was conscious that I was alone at the bar, standing in my stupid dress clearly twenty years younger than everyone else in the room. I was just starting my second glass of Belle Epoque when I heard a calmly familiar voice at my side.

"And what aspect of Asian relief particularly interests you the most, Miss James?" I practically mouthed his name.

"I was relieved to hear you had escaped," he said quietly.

"Not nearly so relieved as I was."

I turned to face him, his darkly exotic looks were out of place in a room of older, whiter Upper East Side financiers and New York dowagers. And just as it had when we first had dinner together, I felt my anger dissolve and fall away in his actual presence. There was something about him that was calming, reassuring, and a flicker of doubt crossed my mind that I was really capable of what I was being asked to do. I hadn't realized just how relived I would be to see him again There were so many things I wanted to ask him, to tell him, but I remembered we were being overheard. Even so, being near him again and seeing that he was very much alive, I forgot myself and my greeting kiss turned into something else. I reached up and found his mouth, all the relief and joy of seeing him again and knowing that I would feel safer in his arms than I had for days going into my kiss. I knew I was probably attracting attention, but I suddenly just didn't care.

"Wow, that's quite a welcome," he laughed, holding me out to arm's length to look at me, "and quite unexpected I have to say."

"I ... I didn't know if you were even alive," I stared back at him.

"I'm staying here at the hotel; did you want to go to my room? We could talk?"

And there was so much I wanted to talk to him about, but at that moment I couldn't think of how to say it. Or at least how to say it convincingly." Instead I said, "Can we just dance for a minute?"

"You dance?"

"Backwards and in heels," I quipped.

The organizers of the fundraiser had chosen a good band and, with impeccably bad timing, as Jai led me to a less crowded part of the dance floor, they broke into the unbelievably romantic opening bars of *"This Love of Mine."* Jai took me in his arms and, for a moment, I thought I was going to totally lose it. Why fate always seemed to conspire to throw us together in the most romantic settings seemed impossibly unfair, particularly now that I felt the pleasure of the body of the man I was about to betray once again next to mine. He had the kind of perfect rhythm hard to find in a man, and his lead was effortless. Dressed in my beautiful gown and lost for a moment in the Sinatra song, it took everything I had at that moment not to blurt out the truth.

"Well, you're a pretty swell dancer," I remarked, trying to pull myself together.

"Officers' Club. It was required, but frankly I don't have a lot of use for it lately." I made a mental note to remind myself to ask about his military career. It seemed so strange that I felt we had been through a lot together and yet I'd known him for only days. For the moment, though, I just wanted the feel of his arms around me.

"Not that I'm not enjoying the wonderful surprise of your company, Brea, but I have to assume it's not a coincidence we're meeting here tonight?"

"No, but please let me tell you why later."

"If I may say so, you don't quite seem your usual witty self, either. You're not in any danger being with me tonight are you?"

"No, no ... I—" I still wasn't sure exactly what I was going to tell Jai, not sure just how much I *could* tell him, but clearly in the short time we were together he had come to know me better than maybe I knew myself. "Actually, events like these are my regular beat," I lied. "For example, I'm sure Mrs. Kaplan over there gave her husband a thirty-thousand-dollar Rolex for their anniversary five years ago, with a current value around fifty thousand dollars. And I'm betting that lovely couple by the bar own a yacht at the Hamptons for three mill. It's all just business."

"And poor me? With just this tux I had to rent from the concierge. Am I just business, too?" he laughed.

"Hey, I hear you may be a rich man soon. Correction, an even *richer* man."

"I will?"

"Listen, Jai, Dhaka didn't go well for either of us, not to mention what happened at Suaka Awan. If I'm honest, I was also kind of depending on the commission for recovering the Goddess, and yet we both came out of it with nothing." Even as I repeated a script Byrne had made me carefully rehearse earlier, on the inside I was just hating myself for being as much of a cheating, lying asshole to Jai as Scott had been to me.

"I know, and I feel I am myself to blame for that. I had clearly underestimated my opponents, and I would never have forgiven myself if I had put you in danger." I felt his strong hand even more securely on my back. "Sometimes we are encumbered by our principles, Brea, and I'm hoping now that I can still secure a sale—even if it has to be through the black market—then perhaps some of the good from the Goddess can still be realized."

I wanted him to shut up, to stop being so revelatory, conscious of those who would be listening in to our conversation.

"Perhaps there is an alternative, Jai, even now, a way to make it still happen."

He pulled away from me slightly, looking at me questioning. "Why exactly are you here, Brea?"

I took a deep breath "What if I could show you a way that a deal for the Goddess could still be possible?" I didn't wait for his reply but continued in a rush. "Bowden and Lowe have assured me it could. If the Goddess is still on the market, and you're really still looking for a buyer, I can that make it happen."

"No, no. Absolutely not. There was a breach of intelligence, someone knew about the earlier arrangement, someone with ... resources."

"I know that now, and they know ... *they* know, too, Jai," I said quickly. "It was someone in the Pakistani Intelligence they said, the IS ... something?"

"ISI," he said. "But who's 'they?'" he questioned.

"I have people too, you know, Jai."

"Your friend from Interpol perhaps?" I tensed but then remembered he had known about my first meeting with Byrne in Dhaka.

"Turns out I'm a girl who needs friends after all," I conceded.

"And to what extent are your 'friends' involved in this new deal?"

I shook my head. "Not at all. Any transaction you agree to will be just between you and, if you trust me, ... me. The money is still on the table. They really want the figurine, and they really want to buy it from you."

I sensed Jai digesting this, but I pushed on. "This can happen Jai—you can get the money you need and then you can buy all the arms, ammunition and explosives you want," I found myself saying.

"Why would you say that?"

"Well, isn't that's what's on your shopping list, Jai?"

"Yes, actually, it is."

"So, the crock you gave me about empowering women, funding schools and overhauling healthcare?" I knew I was going dangerously off script with this, but even just saying it made me remember I was still angry with him.

"That's the only way it happens. Under the current regime, the only way it *can* happen. Things will have to change; blood will be spilled. I don't have the luxury of living in a democracy, Brea."

I brushed that aside. "Anyway, that's why I'm here. This is the message I was told to deliver."

"Told by whom, Brea?"

"My clients are ... connected. Purchasing antiquities always requires some political and diplomatic maneuvering, not to mention some really good knowledge about the background of the sale and the motivations of the seller. To them, this one is no different."

I felt Jai wince, almost unconsciously scanning the ballroom before turning his attention back to me.

"And you believe them?"

"Yes. Yes, Jai, I really do."

"And this is how you knew I would be here?"

"Well, I would never have found out from your Instagram page," I said trying to lighten the interrogation. Byrne had certainly prepared me well, like a pro, but I felt Jai looking at me carefully, trying to determine a deceit, a betrayal. I could only imagine he was skilled at detecting when people were lying to him.

I was relieved when he held me close again, but he said, "Well, I suppose it makes a change for you from trying to secure the policy for Mr. Kaplan's Rolex," he sighed. "You know, trust a steep cliff from which to fall, Brea," he whispered in my ear.

"That it is, Mr. Khan, that it is."

I was aware that the song had finished, perhaps some time ago, and the two of us were alone in the middle of the deserted dance floor. If he was aware of it, Jai didn't take his eyes off of mine. From his silence, it was clear he wanted me to make up my own mind about what happened next.

Finally, I said, "Weren't you going to take me to your room?"

"Won't you shower with me, darling?" I said lazily, sometime later.

To my surprise, and actual relief, being with Jai again had been easy. What started with hatred for him lying to me about the use of the money had become diluted to a mutual understanding laced with some mistrust. Now, after we had been together again, I even felt some of the trust had returned that we had shared back in *Suaka Awan*. Whatever our individual, private motives were, it seemed that neither of us could wait until we could get to the privacy of his room and, in contrast to the languid, amatory seduction in Bangladesh, no sooner was the door closed than he was kissing me passionately. He quickly found the long zipper of my gown, and I stepped out of it in just my heels, basking in the way he looked at my body, studying it in a way that I might have found unnerving in any other man. In any other man than him. I didn't feel embarrassed or scrutinized; I just felt adored. While the tension between us was different this time, there was the same assuredness I had felt with him in the jungle. The same sexy confidence that just wholly consumed me. And when he eventually laid me on the bed, I just knew I wanted him in a way that I had never wanted a man before.

Maybe it had been that reminder of the intense intimacy we shared, or maybe I was just tiring of the whole spy game charade, but I now had a clearer idea of what I needed do next. Being back with Jai had emboldened me in a way that had been missing since I had returned to New York, and I now felt I had the confidence to do what felt to me like the right thing. Now, as he slipped into the shower beside me, he smiled and took my hand as I ran the water. Wet, his body was even more magnificent. I traced his scars and injuries, kissing all over his body and running my tongue over wherever I found a bullet wound, a blemish or anything else on the amazingly rich history of his body. Before I was finished, I couldn't help but be pleasantly surprised to feel his hardness nuzzle against me. But, for now, that really had to wait.

I touched my fingers over his lips and tapped on the glass shower with my fingernail to get his attention. In the foggy condensation of the glass wall I wrote, "*CIA Listening.*"

Annoyingly, he didn't look that surprised; he simply nodded and waited expectantly.

"You trust me?" I mouthed, and I had to wait for what I thought was an infuriatingly long time before he nodded.

I held him close and whispered into his ear. "This is a new game, new allegiances: They want Sajjad and they say they'll support you if you help them find him."

"Sajjad?" he whispered back.

I nodded. His face was expressionless as I revealed this to him, and instead he asked.

"Who hit *Suaka Awan*?"

The directness of his question momentarily floored me. I hesitated before I told him, "Pakistan Intelligence, with a tip from the CIA because they learned that you were behind fucking up their little deal with the statue's previous owner."

"And now?"

"Now, I don't know. I think I trust them—this time they have everything to gain from helping you." Of this hurried resume of everything I had learned in the past few days, he did register surprise. For a while I was quietened, both of us calmed by the warm pulsing of the shower.

Eventually I whispered, "Nothing matters, Jai, nothing matters at all, unless you want to do this."

He nodded, "Anything else I should know?" he mouthed.

"Only that I think I'm falling in love with you."

At this last piece of news, he tilted his head and smiled, raising his eyebrows, making it impossible to know what he was thinking. After what seemed an agonizingly long wait with our eyes locked, neither of us wishing to speak, he kissed me, our lips lightly grazing each other before he kissed me fully and in a way that at that moment I really wanted to feel.

"We'll leave for Mazar-i Sharif tomorrow," he finally announced loudly to no one and anyone listening.

To me he smiled and mouthed the word, "Tonight."

6 | CAIRO

The Gulfstream G650ER's engines were already powered up, a single source of lighted activity in the otherwise darkened airfield. And although it felt like only hours earlier since my confession in the shower, we'd both used the time well, busy laying some elaborate plans. It was still dark out as we had made our way to Teterboro; a nondescript bread delivery truck had been waiting for us outside the same loading bay Byrne had dropped me at just hours earlier. The driver, clearly one of Jai's employees, said barely four words to Khan as we made our way silently out of Manhattan. Before we left, I had asked for the laptop to be delivered to the room, and I powered it up long enough to memorize the IP address and banking codes of the transfer Byrne had given me. Now wearing one of Khan's dress shirts, a beautifully made Turnbull & Asser Bengal blue which I had cinched with one of his more colorful ties, the Tom Ford, along with the laptop, had been left in a dumpster outside of the hotel.

Once we arrived at the airstrip, a ground engineer left the plane and wished us a good flight, as Jai led me to the front of the plane. It was totally unsurprisingly to me that he knew how to pilot a jet.

"Anyone joining us?" I asked, as he gestured to the copilot's seat.

"I sincerely hope not," he grinned. "Now strap in."

"Yes, Captain," I said. "I do hope there's a movie."

Khan confidently prepared the aircraft, speaking calmly and clearly in perfect English with a list of coordinates that I could only guess were probably far from our actual destination. We gained clearance from the control tower, and he immediately powered up the jet to taxi across to the runway.

"Ready?" he asked, when we reached the top of the runway. I nodded, and as he pulled smoothly back on the throttles, the Gulfstream gathered speed, hurtling along the tarmac before smoothly lifting off. From the copilot seat, the experience was exhilarating, the runway lights dropping away and the glow of Manhattan coming immediately into view. In no time, we crossed the narrow strip of the Hudson before turning eastwards. Despite the mixed emotions and excitement of the evening, I felt myself drifting asleep and after an hour or so I was vaguely aware of Jai flicking off the Gulfstream's beacon transponder before powering on over the dark ocean.

It was hard for me to really believe what was happening. I was now somewhere over the Atlantic Ocean in a private jet being piloted by an outlawed tribal leader and gangster whom I had now memorably fucked more than once. As I pushed back my seat, my bare feet propped up on the million-dollar dash of the cockpit; it felt the first time I could really take stock of what was happening to me. What had been a simple work assignment had now exploded into this complex plan of deception and extremely high stakes. The Joni Mitchell line about being a "cog in something turning," of events happening that were much bigger than just me, ran in my mind. And even though I felt I now had better control of my part in the charade, it was impossible to gauge just how pissed off the CIA might be, particularly now that they must be aware of my double-cross. There was so much riding on the success of our mission on all sides and yet, barring a missile attack out of sheer vindictiveness, I felt oddly safe in our flying gin palace.

Running my eyes over the mass of dials and instruments in the darkened cockpit, I also found it hard to underestimate the man next to me. I had wanted to keep him company through the long flight, but even with the excitement happening in my life, I knew I must have dozed several times.

"So where did you learn to fly?" I asked.

"Before my dastardly life of crime, I was a captain in the air force. I have to assure you, though, this thing is much more comfortable than a MiG."

"There's so much I don't know about you," I sighed.

"Is it too late to convince you that I'm really a nice boy?" he almost giggled, "Would it surprise you to know, for example, that I was a boy scout?"

"Sure you were!"

"No, really, I was a boy scout. Technically, I'm Kashmiri, which means from the Northern Tribes of Pakistan, but much of my childhood was spent in England, which is where I was a scout, and also where I attended the Royal Air Force Officer School at Cranwell. When I came home, I really saw my future as a pilot and I had hopes I could help build the kind of professional air force that I had seen in Europe. Later, when the fighting seemed over, I thought maybe I would fly civilian aircraft, as the Gulf States were just establishing their own national airlines and were crying out for pilots. I would start a family, live well in Dubai or Abu Dhabi. I thought my future really was mapped out.

"But the fighting didn't stop?"

"No, it didn't stop and then my father was killed by the Russians during the occupation of Afghanistan. My mother and my four sisters were killed in a rocket attack by the Taliban in 1995, so you see I really became a man without allegiance, a man without a country, but my parents at least really did try to raise me well."

"You're still a boy scout, Jai—still trying to do the right thing. I don't understand the politics of your people, or why you need the arms, but I do know you're trying to create a better future for them."

He shrugged, gesturing to the blackness outside of the cockpit. "Perhaps who we are and where we come from is nothing *but* a political statement. Everyone else benefits from war—the politicians, the religious leaders, the foreign interests—but it's the people who suffer. The people always suffer, so yes, I'd like to change that. Or die trying," he laughed.

Despite his flight skill, I knew the plane was largely capable of flying itself, and I wanted to take advantage of my time with him alone and make up for my earlier deceit.

"Did you know I was planted by the CIA?" I said eventually.

"I had hoped you weren't, but yes, the coincidence was troubling. Plus, you seemed suddenly very knowledgeable about regional politics for someone who keeps doing her best to convince me she is just an insurance loss adjuster."

"I know, and I'm honestly sorry, Jai. I wouldn't have agreed if I didn't think some good might finally come from this. It was all so frightening, so confusing—a whole government trying to deceive you into forgetting the truth, the knowledge that you could be responsible for hurting the very people who had tried so hard to protect you. I couldn't sit back and just take part in something I knew would put you in danger."

"And they told you that wouldn't happen?"

"No, no, they didn't, but I honestly believe it's a plan that could work. Everything you had told me at *Suaka Awan*—your hopes for the people, the country—I believe this stupid deal could still help make that happen."

"It might," he agreed, "but it's risky. It's risky for you, too, Brea, and I'm not so sure I want to take that risk with your life."

"Just worry about your guy, this Siraj Sajjad," I said, not quite as confident as I sounded.

Ahead of us I could faintly see a thin ribbon of dawn from the east, and large billowy clouds suggesting we were nearing land.

"Where are we?"

"Northern Morocco, Spain, is over here to the left." As the sky lightened, I could see fishing boats on the straits below us, and, as we crossed over land an occasional town or city seemed to pass soundlessly beneath us. I could also tell after a sleepless night he was tiring.

"Could I fly this thing?" I asked.

"I don't doubt that *you* could," he smiled, yawning. "Why?"

"We're on an important mission here; I really can't have you crashing us into the sea. But I have something that might keep you awake."

I leaned over and kissed him. Relishing the softness of his lips, the willingness of his mouth, my hand drifted to his cock and I smiled at the stiffening eagerness in his pants.

"Well, good morning, Savior of the People," I murmured.

I unzipped him, slipping my hand around him and massaged his cock. "You know, I really didn't properly take advantage of this magnificence in the shower last night," I sighed.

"Brea ... " he groaned softly, not taking his eyes off of the sky, "I really don't think ... "

I silenced him as I released my seatbelt and knelt, taking him fully in my mouth. As my tongue encircled him, I felt the plane lurch a little.

"Does this thing have autopilot?" I murmured, momentarily glancing up at him. He nodded, flicked a few switches on the control panels of the plane, then leaned back in his seat.

"Now then, we can properly concentrate on keeping you awake," I said. Still wearing his oversize shirt, I was easily available to him and slid over his thighs, guiding him easily into my already wet pussy.

"Brea, I still need to see where we're going ..." he breathed.

"Oh, I think you can feel your way," I whispered back as I slid more firmly on his rigid cock. I opened my shirt and cupped my breasts invitingly for him as I felt his hands explore my body, tentatively at first, and then with greater passion. And as I moved slowly on him I felt his cock thickening even more inside of me, and luxuriated in the feeling of him stretching me, pushing deeply into secret places. His thrusts were now matching my downward plunges and I encouraged him, willing him with softly spoken obscenities in his ear. Somewhere deep inside me, with an origin I couldn't understand, I felt a rising wave of pleasure rolling over me, and I felt him stiffen, and his breathing coming in gasps. I closed my eyes as he finally erupted deep inside me as the brilliance of the Mediterranean daybreak flooded the cockpit.

The jet came in fast, the rising sun glinting off our wings. Having left the ocean behind, Jai began a long, slow decent that made my ears erupt. The radio, which had been silent or limited to brief hushed murmurs during the night, crackled into life, and Jai responded in short to and fro conversations in aviation navigation code. Now, and lower over the land, we seemed to just skim above scattered palms and small communities as the ground came closer. Despite the early hour, the heat of the desert seemed palpable, shimmering under our wings, although as Jai lowered the undercarriage, the landscape became increasingly more urban. Streets, houses, delivery trucks, the awakenings of an early morning city flashed by.

"Where are we, Jai?"

"Egypt."

"Egypt? We need to refuel?"

He shook his head, distractedly concentrating on the controls. "I just need to pick something up."

The wide stretch of smooth tarmac suddenly appeared under the wings and we landed, still at speed. Jai applied the brakes, gently at first and then more firmly as the plane slowed to a taxiing speed. After our lonely night over the ocean, it seemed as if we were suddenly surrounded by the world, with the massive jets of every nation's airline dwarfing us as we joined taxi queues to the airport terminal. Unlike most of the traffic headed to the airport's major terminals, he instead guided our aircraft to a hangar a discrete distance from the main building, and where he finally brought the plane to a stop.

Cairo was a surprise. I thought we were flying directly to Mazar-i Sharif as he had indicated, but Jai seemed to be following some already well-thought-out plan, which seemed evident when we opened the aircraft's door and a uniformed officer greeted us, smartly saluting and exchanging greetings with Jai in Arabic. There seemed to be no formal immigration process, just a brief exchange that included Jai being given a small package, as we were simply escorted to a waiting van.

If I had thought traffic was bad in Dhaka, it paled by comparison to the chaos of Cairo. Where the streets weren't clogged with traffic busying with the day's business, the locals drove like contestants in a competitive racetrack. After a mercifully short yet hair-raising ride, I couldn't have been more relieved when we turned into the stately entrance of the InterContinental Cairo Semiramis.

Being with Jai Khan, I was realizing, was an opportunity to enjoy the kind of elevated status reserved for celebrities or national leaders. No sooner had we entered the hotel lobby than the property manager and a small coterie of hotel staff anxiously greeted us, swiftly escorting us to a private elevator. As with the official at the airport, Jai seemed to take this respectful fawning in his stride, politely declining the invitations to enjoy any of the privileged amenities reserved for VIPs. Our suite, however, seemed like a palace. The series of beautifully appointed rooms lacked for nothing, decorated with freshly cut flowers, overflowing bowls of fruit and gifts, and when the curtains were automatically opened, they revealed stunning views of the Nile, the span of the river broad and sparkling as it flowed through the city right below our window.

Graciously dispatching our hosts, Jai immediately returned to matters at hand. Opening the envelope he had been given at the airport, he shook out a phone and some money, leaving a large bulky object in place.

"Care package?" I asked curiously.

"Something like that."

Among the contents of the envelope was a credit card, which he gave to me.

"Shopping. You'll need clothes." He pointed to his dress shirt that I was still wearing as an improvised shirtdress. "Maybe something a little more modest," he said awkwardly.

"Is it stolen?"

"No, it's not stolen," he said exasperatedly, "It's actually mine, so please just buy anything you need."

He powered up the phone, excused himself and immediately began a series of deeply involved conversations in Arabic. I took the opportunity to freshen up, and then, as he was still engrossed on the phone, decided to run down to the lobby. I quickly found a helpful concierge who directed me to a nearby mall where I could buy a change of clothes without attracting too much attention.

The mall was really an extension of the hotel shops and a curious mixture of familiar Western retailers and local Egyptian stalls selling Arabic clothing and imported goods along with souvenirs for the tourists. Although it was barely mid-morning I was surprised how busy it was, the cafes and food courts buzzed with conversations in so many different languages while the stores were doing a brisk trade with tourists and young affluent Egyptians equally. It was strangely liberating being on my own, and I realized it was the first time since I had landed in Dhaka all those weeks ago that I was in a foreign city without Jai or Aliyah by my side. Maybe it was because of that I felt a new sense of vulnerability, an eerie feeling of exposure, and not just because of the improvised shirt dress I was wearing. I had the distinct feeling I was being watched. I hastily ducked into the first boutique I saw and quickly found a pair of jeans and T-shirt to replace Jai's dress shirt. It was only when I came out of the first boutique, already with several shopping bags, that in my peripheral vision I noticed a man who I thought I had seen in the hotel lobby. I told myself it probably wasn't that unusual; I was sure many of the hotel guests shopped nearby, but his well-tailored dark suit and sunglasses were distinctive among the groups of casually dressed tourists and the more traditional clothes of the local Egyptians. I saw his reflection in the glass window of a shoe shop and when I stopped by a stall selling scarves, he was still right behind me. I waited until I was in the safety of a large crowd, with two policemen lounging on a railing nearby, when I abruptly turned and confronted him.

"Why are you following me?"

He seemed surprised, as much by the question as being discovered.

"Because I was told to—it is my job, madame," he almost stammered in a thick Arabic accent.

"Who told you to follow me?"

"My boss, madame."

"What is their name?"

He hesitated before stammering, "Jai Khan, madame, of course."

I gestured to a table near a fountain. "Sit down."

"This I cannot do under any circumstances, madame."

"Why?"

"Because I am supposed to follow you in secret."

I sighed. Close up he was little more than a kid. Late teens or early twenties at most, and he appeared more nervous around me than I felt frightened of him.

"Can you at least tell me your name?"

"It is Abasi, madame."

"Okay, Abasi, you can help me spend your boss's money."

"No, this I cannot do. Jai Khan pays me very well; my sister goes to college because of his kindness. I cannot steal from him."

"It's not stealing. It's helping, Abasi." He brightened a little at this, and listened keenly as I told him the list things I needed.

"Here is too expensive, Madame," he said thoughtfully, once I'd told him the list. "I must show you better place."

It seemed I had only followed Abasi a short distance out of the mall, but the streets and squares we entered were a world away from the glitzy Western-style designer shops around the hotel. The bustling souk he had led me to was a seemingly disorganized maze, a jumble of merchandizing where electrical emporiums rubbed shoulders with fashion boutiques, jewelry stores and coffee shops. Abasi confidently led me through the labyrinth to a shop that seemed to specialize in imported merchandise and I quickly chose a 4.80 GHz Turbo Boost Lenovo ThinkPad, which would probably be up to the task I required. A separate router was harder to find, but we eventually unearthed a Sierra Wireless AirLink and, in the same shop, a change of warmer clothes for traveling and a burner phone with a detachable Nighthawk LTE Mobile Hotspot. Although I was mostly pleased with the morning's shopping spree, with the exhaustive negotiations over price and the necessary but interminable breaks for tea, the whole thing took longer than I would have liked. I felt reassured with Abasi beside me even in this most Western of Arabic cities, as the merchants clearly had less interest in negotiating with a woman, wanted instead to sell me jewelry or perfume, and I was sure his influence helped the most stubborn store owners agree to a more favorable deal.

It was with more than a sense of relief that Abasi eventually dropped me back at the hotel, both of us laden with the fruits of our morning in the souk. I thanked him for his patience and, much to his embarrassment, stole a warm hug before I was waved down by one of the hotel staff to tell me Jai was in the restaurant and had asked me to join him.

I was shown to an outside table on the patio overlooking the river but, as Jai was still busily engaged on his phone, it gave me a minute to take in the spectacular view of the Nile. Spanning the river was the Corniche Qasr al-Nil Bridge, almost overshadowing the restaurant patio, while beneath it, large cruise ships vied with commercial barges and smaller dhows on the bustling waterway. The prospect of lunch also reminded me that I hadn't eaten since before the fundraiser where I had met Jai over twenty-four hours earlier, and I ordered the heavily recommended cheeseburger and fries.

When he got off the phone, he looked irritated. "Where were you? I was getting worried."

"Well, you could have always asked Abasi, I guess."

He sighed. "So much for discrete surveillance."

"He was a very sweet man, very helpful."

"I chose him because he could disarm and kill any kidnappers, not to help you pick out matching outfits," he said patiently.

"Is this what it's going to be like with you? I'm going to need bodyguards everywhere I go?"

"People can come after me with everything they've got, and that's the path I've chosen, but I won't stand for the people I care about being included in that."

"I should warn all my boyfriends."

"Boyfriends? I'll need their names and contact information," he said with faux gruffness. "I'll tear out their hearts myself."

"Jai!"

"Kidding! Really, I have no idea how to do that."

I nodded to his phone, "What's up? You looked worried."

"There's been a complication," he said, the terseness returning to his voice.

"What was it you're here to get, Jai?"

He gave me a strange look and didn't answer right way.

"The Goddess," he said eventually.

"It's here?"

"It is."

"Why?"

"Because the person who has it is here."

I was immediately aware of something like confused anger raising within me. "But you told me *you* had it," I said slowly, watching his face.

"I told you I was in a *position* to get it."

"So you entered into a deal with me, with my clients, with my country for something you don't actually own?"

"Yet."

"I fucking trusted you, Jai."

People glanced our way at what they must a thought must have been no more than a lover's tiff.

"I know. I know, and I'm sorry. Things don't always have the happy way of working out here. My contact is not the legal owner— he never was. Arrangements were made to ensure its retrieval back in Pakistan, but he fled here, which is why *we* are here."

"So how is it I'm not talking to him?"

"The Syrian? Because he's nobody. A low-level sometime politician and full-time crook. Don't make the same mistake your friends at the CIA made; he has no interest in doing good for anyone unless there's a huge profit in it for him!"

"But he has the Goddess!"

"He stole it!"

"Now you're stealing it!" Many heads in the restaurant were now turned our way, while the maître d' nervously clutched a menu and assiduously tried not to look over to our table.

Honestly, I didn't care. "Don't give me all that 'things are different here' shit," I ranted. "The truth is the truth. Trust is trust. We are partners!" I hissed at him. Mercifully, he didn't mention my own deception in New York.

"It made sense to secure a buyer—I'm sure you can bear witness as to how hard that's turned out to be—before securing the figurine."

"So, what do we do now?"

"We get it back."

Lunch was completed in silence and afterwards, the elevator ride back to our room seemed to take an eternity. While our fellow passengers chatted excitedly about their morning at Giza and the wonder of the Pyramids, Jai and I stood awkwardly at opposite sides of the elevator.

"Brea, I honestly didn't mean to deceive you in any way," Jai began once we got back into our room.

"Save it, Jai. I honestly don't want to hear it," I barked back. He followed me into the bathroom as I began washing up and stood at the doorway watching me helplessly.

I didn't want to argue anymore, but didn't want to forgive him either. "Listen, you haven't slept in two days, just get some sleep, okay?" To my complete surprise he sheepishly complied and when I came back into the room he was already in bed, his breathing even and deep.

I was too upset and angry to be anywhere near him so I took my packages to the adjoining room and assembled the computer, removing the tracking software from it first, and then did the same with the phone. I then powered up both the laptop and phone and quickly checked the transfer information without logging on to email or the hotel's server. By the time I had finished setting everything up it was getting dark outside and Jai was still sleeping soundly in the other room, but I was still strangely wired. I wasn't sure if I was still mad at Jai, or whether something else was nagging me—excitement at what he and I were planning to do? fear of failing and the consequences I would invariably face from my own government if we *did* fail?

All of that impenetrable jumble of thoughts was now inextricably mixed up with my own feelings for the man sleeping in the other room. Was my declaration of love the other night foolish considering I barely knew him? Why had I missed him so much, and why did it always feel so right when I *was* with him? Eventually I called down to room service and ordered a snack and coffee and when it arrived, I bummed a cigarette from the waiter. I hadn't smoked since college, and then only barely, but it seemed needed to help me figure out what exactly I was feeling. Taking the tray out to the balcony, I drank and smoked for some time, wondering what on earth I was doing here, watching the river and the sounds of the Cairo, the night falling in a soft indigo blanket over the ancient city.

The next morning, I found I was still simmering from our first row and it didn't help that now, barely light, Jai was telling me to quickly pack as we were leaving immediately.

"Where are we going?" I asked sulkily.

"To fulfill a promise," he said.

"Oh, something different then," I sniped.

Outside, on the hotel forecourt a rented car was waiting for us, and Jai drove a short way along the Cornish, on our left, the surface of the Nile burnished gold, busying to greet the day, before heading into a jumble of neighborhoods. The streets quickly narrowed, the houses huddling closer together, as we drove deeper into the neighborhoods, eventually stopping in a quiet alley. Although I had no idea what this negotiation would be like, I assumed we were waiting to rendezvous with the Syrian.

Jai quickly scanned the alley and neighboring houses then slipped out of the car. "I'll be back in a minute," he said.

After a short while he returned with a package of delicious smelling wrapped paper which he handed to me.

"What's this?"

"A peace offering? Breakfast—it's *hawawshi*. I've noticed you get cranky when you're hungry," he grinned. He was trying to get back in my good books, but he'd have to do better than this.

"I do not get cranky," I sniffed, unwrapping the package of warm dough stuffed with an unbelievably tantalizing mixture of meat and onions, hot peppers and fragrant fresh herbs.

Jai was presumably prepared for a long wait, and the atmosphere in the car had all the air of a stakeout.

"What are we doing here Jai?"

"Waiting."

"For what?"

"For the right time."

I continued eating, "So, if we're in Egypt," I said between mouthfuls, "why is he called the Syrian?"

"You know, you do ask an awful lot of questions, Brea," he teased.

"Because it's the only way I can find out what's going on."

"He's called the Syrian because he comes from Syria, and his name is Haamid ibn Faheem ibn Ghazawwi."

"Okay, so shorter," I agreed.

We waited another thirty minutes or so, Jai never taking his eyes off the alley. I completed breakfast, noisily scrunching the paper just to break the silence.

"So, he stole the Goddess?"

"Technicality, he stole the Goddess from the people who stole the Goddess. Ever since it was stolen from the National Museum, recent history hasn't been kind to your statue."

"And why do you need it so badly?"

"I think you know the answer to that," he said dryly.

"No, I mean you're a millionaire already, couldn't you just fund your uprising yourself?" I found myself echoing the same question Byrne had asked me less than a week ago.

Jai gave me one of those deep searching looks before eventually deciding I was honestly interested in his answer.

"I could," he said softly, "but we'll need friends. Even if we are successful in overthrowing the corrupt government, that's just the first step along a very long road." I saw him glance at both of the wing mirrors to check any activity behind us and then his eyes rested again on the house across the alley. "Our whole infrastructure has been neglected, telecommunications, civic structure, schools, hospitals. I'm not even sure if I can guarantee food security for a nation of people who have been starved for centuries. Our first evening together, you asked me why I was so eager to sell the Goddess and why would I not prefer her to remain in my country. Do you remember that?"

I nodded.

"I need friends, Brea, powerful friends, so no, I'm not just asking the Goddess to raise money for us. I'm asking her to build a relationship with your country—I really can't do it without their investment, without their support." I wasn't sure I had ever seen this side of him before, even at *Suaka Awan*. Honest, vulnerable and trusting in the way he described all this to me. I was about to reach my hand out to him, when he suddenly stiffened, his eyes even more intently focused on the house across the alley.

"Can you drive?" he asked.

"Is that a question?"

"I need you to drive when I come back," he said patiently.

"I learned to drive in New York City. I think I can handle it"

I sensed something about to happen, and Jai slipped out of the car. "Start the engine, and you might want to leave it running," he barely whispered.

"What is this, a bank heist?" I said rolling my eyes with mock drama.

"Just leave it running. We're on a tight schedule and might have to leave in a hurry." And with that, he was gone, moving swiftly across the street and disappearing behind a wall next to the house he had been watching.

I slid across to the driver's seat and started the car. The sun was now rising higher, above the rooftops, and I was grateful for the air-conditioning, amazed how hot the car quickly became. Waiting there in the alley, I watched some kids playing soccer in the street while I distractedly fiddled with the radio trying to find some Western news or music. After less than fifteen minutes, Jai emerged, walking briskly.

He got into the passenger seat and simply said, "Drive."

"How did it go ... ?" I began.

"We really might want to go now, Brea," Jai said.

I pulled out of the alley and into the traffic of a broader street as almost immediately a car burst out of a nearby garage a block away, followed by another.

"What happened in there? What did they say?"

"They didn't say much, nothing at all, actually—and you might want to drive a little faster."

"But you must have seen somebody?"

"No, that was rather the idea.

"So you did steal it!"

"*They* stole it; I'm reclaiming it," he corrected.

We were now leaving the neighborhood on a busier street. "And you just stole it back? What a bunch of thieves!" I yelled, throwing my hands in the air.

"I can't actually argue with you there, Brea, but please keep your hands on the steering wheel. Okay, left here."

I swung the car, dipping into a narrow alley that emerged onto a bustling square, on the far side of which was a busy market area forcing us to slow down.

"Who's following us?" Jai asked, searching through the same bag he had been given when we arrived in Cairo yesterday.

I glanced in the rearview mirror. "Looks like a white Mercedes and a bunch of guys in a pickup truck.

"Okay, don't worry, we're fine all the time the police are around," Jai said in a voice that I was sure was meant to be reassuring.

"We're fine? We're being chased by a bunch of very angry-looking guys you've just stolen from and we're fine?" He was right, though, I had never seen such a noticeable police presence, as though they were preparing for a parade, a major sporting event—or a coup. At nearly every junction uniformed police or army vehicles were parked or gathered in groups, and everywhere they were trying to direct the chaotic traffic.

Even though there were several vehicles between us, the throng of market-goers forced me to drive slower and slower.

"It's okay to use your horn, New York girl," he teased. I was amazed he could be so calm while being the subject of a car chase, albeit a slow motion one. Eventually we ground to a complete halt as a cart loaded with textiles had pulled around in front of us.

"I can't pass them," I exclaimed in frustration, thumping the steering wheel.

"In just a few yards, there's a narrow alley on the left, "Jai said calmly. "It's going to be tight, but I think we'll be able to get through."

In the rearview mirror I saw some of the men getting out of the cars and making their way quickly toward us.

"Jai?"

"Here," he indicated to the narrow archway opening to the left now just yards ahead. The cart inched forward painfully slowly as the men behind us broke into a run and quickly closed the gap between us. I nudged the back of the cart and squeezed through the narrow archway, the door mirrors on both sides slicing off neatly with an alarming crunch, while the first men to reach us banged on the trunk of our car before running back to theirs.

"You can go a little faster here. Go right, there." I steered down a hill, a sharp bend at the bottom causing the back of the car to spin out, careening into a market stall and causing the vendors to scatter.

"Let's go," Jai tapped the dashboard as I struggled for control and straightened the car out down the alley.

"How about you just tell me where we're going and let me do the driving, okay?"

To my dismay, in my rearview mirror I saw both cars still somehow managing to follow us. I spun the car back onto a major road, and with Jai's calm voice directing me like some exotic version of Siri, he navigated me through the city.

"Straight ahead. Brake here. You can speed up here."

I was switching from accelerator to brake, palms moist. I prayed we wouldn't get stopped by any traffic cops, although it often seemed that I was driving no more crazily than anyone else on those narrow streets.

We were coming to the outskirts of the city, and I sensed our pursuers moving closer, the two vehicles doggedly following us despite the crazy pace.

"Here, go right," Jai said with his seemingly encyclopedic knowledge of the city. "We're going to go up those steps—you might need a bit more gas."

"You think?" I spun the car wide and bounced up the stone steps, the car bucking wildly as it struggled for purchase on the uneven surface. At the top of the steps, another road opened up.

"Right!"

I swung hard on the wheel and we immediately descended down another narrow alley, people scattering everywhere, my hand on the horn. Finally, we reemerged onto what looked like a major highway out of the city, and the road opened up to us out to the suburbs.

As the traffic thinned, the police became less numerous, and I realized we were only becoming more vulnerable.

"They're still behind us," I yelled. And as if on cue, the car's rear window suddenly shattered, sending shards of glass everywhere as a series of gun shots broke out behind us. I shrieked, the memory of the helicopter attack which I'd been trying so hard to suppress the past few weeks came instantly flooding back.

"They're firing at us!" I yelled.

Jai said nothing, calmly pulling out a gun from the bag between his knees and checking it.

"Okay, you're doing fine, Brea. Up ahead you're going to be turning onto a highway. I want you just to go as fast as you can until I tell you."

The turn came almost immediately and I instinctively swerved onto the entrance ramp nearly rolling the car in the process. Mercifully, there was little traffic on the highway and the car responded smoothly as I floored it, but any hopes that I could outrun them were short lived, as they stayed right behind us, the distance only slightly wider. We were now a mile or so out of the city, the traffic had thinned and I was driving the car flat out.

"Now, slow down."

"Slow down?"

"Brake here. Hard!" he touched my arm.

I pressed the brake and we skidded along the highway, fishtailing in a cloud of dust. I struggled to keep the car straight, veering first to the left then, as I over compensated, the back swinging back out alarmingly.

"Perfect," Jai whispered under his breath and swung open his door. Leaning backwards, he fired a volley into the closing Mercedes.

"Now!"

The car kangarooed as I pressed the accelerator all the way down. In the mirror the Mercedes behind us seemed to swerve uncontrollably before rolling spectacularly, parts of the car ripping off like missiles on each impact. It finally came to rest as a pile of crushed metal, enveloped by a thick cloud of dust. However, there was no time for us to high-five, like characters in a caper movie, as out of the dust the pickup truck continued right behind us. I had gained more speed, and the distance between us gradually increased, but any thought that they might abandon the chase evaporated the longer they followed us. The traffic had now thinned out to the extent that at times we were the only two vehicles on the highway, and my heart sank when in the distance, I could just make out two military vehicles, carefully parked to block both lanes.

"Jai?"

He carefully scrutinized the roadblock then slowly said, "Drive around them."

"Is it an army roadblock? Won't they stop us?"

"No, it's the police, just keep driving," Jai said calmly.

It was obvious that several of the officers were out of the vehicles, all of them masked, all of them heavily armed, and as we came closer I could see their weapons aimed at us, one looking like a rocket launcher.

"They're going to kill us!" I yelled.

"It's okay, drive around!" he repeated.

I half closed my eyes, expecting at any minute to hear the bullets rip into the car, and us, or for everything to end in one earth-shattering fiery explosion. But unbelievably the police did nothing as I hurtled through the narrow opening between the two vehicles.

Behind me I saw the truck following us brake hard and swerve in the road, then attempt to reverse. A second later I heard the whoosh of the rocket launcher being fired and the truck almost immediately burst into flames.

"Friends of yours?" I murmured, my eyes never leaving the road for a second.

"For now, yes."

We drove several more miles further in silence before Jai directed me off the highway to a narrow track leading to a flat plain and there, solitary against the skyline, I was hardly surprised to see the Gulfstream parked alone, waiting for us.

Driving through some rusty gates and past a collection of derelict buildings, it seemed we were on some kind of abandoned airfield and I skidded to a stop several yards away from the jet, getting shakily out of the car almost before it stopped. I was trembling and sweating, my clothes and body covered in fine red dust. For a moment I thought I was going to vomit.

"You were amazing, Brea ..." I heard Jai say behind me.

"Fuck you!" I turned and yelled at him. "Just fuck you. This is fucking bullshit, Jai; it's just one thing after another and it stops now."

"Brea ... "

"Did you kill him?" I asked hysterically.

"Kill who?"

"That guy back there!"

"I'm not sure; I was aiming for the radiator, maybe a lucky shot to the tires."

"Not them, the other one. The Syrian, the one you stole from."

He was silent for a moment. "No, I didn't kill the Syrian, Brea."

"Are you lying? Lying to me again? Because that's what you do, that's what you all do—you, Johnathan fucking Byrne, the CIA, all of you! I know you're a thief; I just have to understand if you're a killer, too."

He held up his hands. "Those guys on the road—no one innocent died today, Brea, you have to believe me."

"And who decides that? Jai Khan, the thief? Jai Khan, the terrorist? Or Jai Khan, the murderer?

"You're right, I did steal from the Syrian, but I told you, the man is worthless. He took bribes; he had no loyalty to his people or to our history," he said dismissively. "And he was in no position to contest ownership of this."

He reached into his jacket and pulled out a small object wrapped in cloth, placing it gently in my hands. I unwrapped it haphazardly, thinking it was perhaps another gun or some other tool of destruction. It took me perhaps a full minute to realize what I was holding in my hands was the Sarianidi Goddess.

"All of it for this?" I asked quietly. "The raid on *Suaka Awan*, that whole charade in New York, those men back there, dead all because of this?"

Jai shook his head. "No, Brea, she is as innocent of any of that as you are." He held me almost cautiously, his hands on my shoulders, consoling, like a favorite uncle, not a lover. "But we should be going."

The interior of the plane was stifling, and I waited outside as Jai prepared the Gulfstream, grateful at least for some breeze coming across the open desert, clutching the ancient statue in my lap as if it were an amulet. I felt tired beyond mere exhaustion, tired of the deceitful spy craft, of names I couldn't pronounce, of being unable to trust anyone, even those I really wanted to trust. I also felt tired of trying to love Jai Khan. The more time I spent with him, the more I realized I had no idea who he was. A man who could flaunt immigration laws, who could shoot with deadly accuracy, who knew people who drove bread delivery vans in Manhattan and could move jets around for him in the desert. Someone who commanded luxury suites in hotels yet could get the police to kill for him; someone who stayed alive only by luck, by his wits and by staying one step ahead of what seemed like a whole laundry list of people wanting to kill him. He appeared at the doorway, the gun in his hand, and he almost casually fired a single round into the gas tank of the car. It ignited into a fireball in seconds.

"It's bearable in here now, Brea, you should come inside," he said softly.

"That's debatable," I said to his face as he helped me aboard.

We took the same places in the cockpit as we had so recently when we left New York. But the mood was different. All the excitement, the certainly of doing the right thing, now gone.

"Where are we going?"

"I think that's rather up to you," he said.

"Me?"

"You have the Goddess now. You have what you came for, the reason you came to Dhaka is in your hands. By any standards, your contract has been fulfilled."

"Then take me home, please, just do that."

"That's fair," he said simply. He quickly completed readying the aircraft and we started slowly taxiing out onto the empty airstrip. At the top of the runway, I asked him to stop. I needed to think. We sat there, both of us gazing at the heat haze at the end of the desolate, sunbaked runway. The hiss of the air conditioning and the sound of the engines muted, the burning car off to our left turning the sky oily black, the aircraft quietly vibrating as if hesitating, waiting. I thought of Scott, and the lengths that had been taken to first ensure my silence, then to orchestrate this whole deal, where I had somehow become the central figure, the person who was going to make it work, or not. I thought of Aliyah's words to me on the broad patio of the Sanctuary of Clouds while teaching me *Pinkat Silat:* "It's never ever over until you say it is." I was beginning to understand that this was a world of deceit and opacity. Nothing was ever as it seemed, but whatever this was, it certainly wasn't over by a long way.

"Okay" I said eventually.

"Okay, what?"

"We go on. Let's get this thing done."

"You know you don't have to."

"That's not quite true, Jai. There's the small matter of the money. If I don't complete our deal, I think we both know I can never go home. I've had a taste of what these people are capable of—they'll ruin my life, Jai. Meanwhile, in your country the fighting will continue; thousands of people are going to continue to live in fear and misery; thousands more will die."

"I'm not sure that's all on you, Brea."

"So you know the codes?"

"What codes?"

"The routing codes the FBI gave me."

"You can tell them to me."

"And you routinely move money around the planet?"

"Yes, actually. We don't do it in paper bags, Brea."

"And the authentication codes, that confirm it's me moving the money and not some hacker?"

"You can teach me."

"He'll know. Sajjad will know. You'll be killed and, I'm betting, he'll eventually find me and the money, too, so you can fuck this up or I can just do it for you. We've come this far, all these people have already died and if we don't at least try to complete the deal with Sajjad, I know neither one of us will ever stop thinking about it."

"And you're sure you want this?"

"Do you remember what you said to me, that first night in *Suaka Awan*, about how you envied me being so sure about everything?"

"I remember."

"Well, that's bullshit. I'm not sure about anything anymore. Nothing makes sense to me since I met you. The only way I get my sanity back is if we go on."

Jai looked at me for a long time before taking my hand. As if creating some symbolic gesture, he placed my hand on the throttles and covering them with his, eased gently back. The aircraft immediately moved, gathering speed as it hurtled across the desert runway and within a few moments, we were in the air, heading east.

7 | THE NORTHERN PROVINCES

We had entered Egypt anonymously like thieves. When we landed in Mazar-i Sharif, it was as rock stars. Waiting on the tarmac were two, shiny-black Mercedes Saloons and an Escalade, all driven by smartly dressed young men in dark sunglasses, all blatantly carrying weapons.

Jai eased the plane to a halt in front of the convoy of vehicles. Powering down the engines he pushed away from his seat, stretched, yawned and smiled, *"Awa 'ahlaan eaziziuny,"* he said. "Welcome darling."

"Quite the homecoming," I murmured. "What exactly have I let myself in for?"

My mood had lifted since leaving Cairo, and my first impressions of Mazar-i Sharif also served to brighten it. It was immediately a distinctly different kind of city from Cairo, which felt almost cosmopolitan in comparison. I could feel their similarly ancient histories; it was in the walls, in the markets, even on the faces of the people, but Mazar pulled from the east, not the Mediterranean Arabic roots of Egypt. Here, many of the roads were barely paved, donkeys shared the highway with noisy, honking Toyota pickups. Bazaars were bustling and crowded, and the dazzling architecture of the Blue Mosque seemed to dominate every skyline. Speeding down dusty boulevards or snaking through its narrow streets, it was impossible not to draw attention to our little convoy, and outside our window, people would shout Jai's name in greeting. Women, darkly dressed in *Chadors,* shyly waved and smiled at us, and more alarmingly to me, guns were fired into the air, often very close to the cars, although ignored by Jai's men.

"I think I've underestimated your popularity here," I told him.

"I'm really not that popular—not like Justin Bieber," he laughed.

He was different here. Lighter among his own people and more relaxed.

We drove across the city to a more suburban area where the houses were further apart, boasting lush gardens and impressive architecture and protected behind impressive walls and gated entrances. We pulled into one of the largest of these, seemingly a small city within itself. Well-armed guards surrounded the walls, while women and children played in the large central courtyard, laid out with Islamic symmetry into four smaller squares intersected with water features and inviting places to sit and gather shaded by fig trees. The effect was that of a cooling, ordered sanctuary within the hurly-burly of the city outside. Descending from the steps of the main building, a tall, elegant man stepped up to greet us. He kissed his brother enthusiastically on both cheeks, before turning to me, his hand on his chest in greeting. "I am Haafiz, the brother of Jai Khan," he explained. "This is my wife, Nazneen," he gestured to a woman behind him in traditional *parahaan* over loose pants, her hair informally covered by a scarf. He was older than his brother, sporting a well-kept salt and pepper beard, cut close, while Jai was clean shaven, but when Haafiz's face broke into a broad smile I could immediately see the resemblance between the two men. "You are welcome in my home, Miss James, please come in."

Apparently, a feast had been organized for that night. Delicious smells of spices and herbs were already permeating through the house from the kitchen where staff were preparing meals only usually prepared for public holidays or religious festivals, to mark the gathering of the two brothers. The unusual inclusion of a tall blonde American woman to the proceedings seemed only to add to the celebratory nature of the proceedings, and Nazneen, in a mixture of broken English and hand gestures, made sure all the facilities of her household were placed at my disposal. She had shown me to where we were going to stay the night, a bright, airy room on the villa's second floor, with an adjoining bathroom, itself an amazing delight. Intricate tiling lined the walls with geometric designs interlaced with delicate flowers and vines that I mused would surely make the centerfold layout in *Architectural Digest* were it in the Hamptons or Bel Air. Someone with prior knowledge of our arrival had filled a large tub scented with rose water and Nazneen left me to soak off the dust from our journey from Egypt. I wasn't home, these were not my people, but relaxing in that beautiful, tranquil sanctuary after the events of the past few days, and listening to the sounds of children playing in the courtyard below and swifts chattering in the eves, I almost felt whole again.

Jai had spent the afternoon catching up with his family and it was only just before dinner that he came up to the room. I was just finishing getting ready, and when he saw me, he was momentarily speechless. I was glad to be out of the dusty clothes I had worn in Cairo and Nazneen had lent me a beautiful kaftan to wear, embroidered with zardozi gold threading under a flowing chador.

"Going native?" he almost gasped.

"I should wear jeans to meet your family?" I teased. But I knew my loose, flowing hair lightly covered by a scarf, and minimal makeup made me look a suitable partner for the younger Khan brother.

The whole family had gathered in a large outside dining area. In addition to Haafiz and Nazneen, I was introduced to a dizzying procession of aunts, uncles, nephews, nieces and family friends before we sat down to the massive table for an unforgettable feast. First came *Ashak*, spicy pasta dumplings stuffed with scallions and served with a delicious tomato sauce, and which Jai showed me how to dip with yogurt and mint garnishes. Then came platters piled high with sizzling, slow-cooked lamb, served with a green hot sauce of garlic, lime juice and chilies. Everything was delicious and although most of the dinner conversation was in Dari, Jai or Haafiz would translate for me. At one point Nazneen spoke to Jai and I saw him remonstrate.

"What is she saying?" I asked him.

"Nothing, it doesn't translate," he replied briskly.

"My wife is saying that you two will have beautiful children," Haafiz interrupted. "If you would be married?" He was obviously warming to this idea and enjoyed teasing his brother.

"Married?" the question confused me momentarily. "To your brother? No!" In my desire to fit in and be an accepted part of Jai's family I really hadn't thought further than that, but everyone clearly found my protests amusing.

"And you're quite sure of this?" he smiled.

"I'm learning not to be sure of anything, Haafiz."

Jai growled something to Haafiz in Dari. I could only recognize the word *baradarm*, brother.

"Please don't listen to this man," Jai said earnestly to me. "My brother was kicked by a goat when he was a kid and sadly has never been the same since."

Watching the two brothers laugh and mock each other, I liked this version of Jai. He was less tense with his family, his smile less ironic.

The feast concluded with piping hot, fried crispy *jalebis* dipped in thick sugary syrup, the delicious dessert seemed to embody how safe and welcomed I felt in the Khan family home.

It was only when I had eaten my fill and laughed with Jai's family that I realized how exhausted I felt from the travel and anticipation of what was to come, and after dinner I excused myself and took Haafiz's suggestion to get some air on the villa's rooftop. Night had fallen over the city, and on the roof the stars looked magnified. Bigger and brighter than I had ever seen them at home, it felt as if I were somehow closer to heaven. Dressed in the kaftan Nazneen had given to me and enjoying the soft Afghan night, it was all too easy to imagine myself as Princess Jasmine, the heroine of some romantic Persian story with Jai Khan as my prince. It was a stupid daydream, and I banished it immediately. This wasn't a fictional Agrabah; it was modern-day Afghanistan, and whatever imagined fantasies I might conjure to comfort myself, the truth was that I was just trying to avoid thinking about the dangers that were to come, the seemingly impossible task Jai and I had set ourselves and how unlikely it was to succeed.

"Beautiful, isn't it?" Haafiz was standing at the entrance to the rooftop nodding over to the view of the city's Blue Mosque, a gorgeously woven Afghan blanket in his hands. "The nights will be getting colder here now; you should take this." I accepted his kindness gratefully and he settled the blanket around my shoulders.

"I was nervous about coming here, to Mazar-i-Sharif," I found myself saying. "It seemed dangerous. I thought I would be out of place."

"And yet, you came. And so perhaps this is your place."

I laughed, "Yes, I came. You probably think I'm crazy."

He shook his head. "Not at all. Look here, we call it the Shrine of Hazrat Ali," he gestured across to the mosque. "We believe it is the tomb of Hazrat-i-Ali Sharif, the cousin and son-in-law of the prophet Muhammad, after whom our city is named."

"It's spectacular, just beautiful, Haafiz," I agreed. "I had never expected anything so spectacular in ..."

" . . . in a city perhaps more well-known now for the destruction and cruelty of our recent past?" he nodded thoughtfully. "That perception doesn't surprise me, Miss James; conflict is, after all, in the very fabric of our city. Alexander the Great explored here, Genghis Khan invaded here, the Russians, the Taliban, they occupied here—this is a land of great warriors and harsh conquerors, but it is also a place of great builders and dreamers. One of our most famous sons is Jalal al-Din Rumi, the poet Rumi, do you know him?

I had a distant memory of an old boyfriend quoting love poetry under the trees outside Healy Hall during my Georgetown days, but I shook my head. "Not well, no."

"'Your task is not to seek for love, but merely to seek and find all the barriers within yourself that you have built against it,'" he quoted.

"That's beautiful Haafiz—that's Rumi?"

"It is, and it explains why we are perhaps all sons of Rumi, why we're all so passionate, such fighters. So determined to find those barriers to love. And perhaps it is one explanation why I don't think you're crazy"

"And your brother? Is he also a son of Rumi?"

He leaned against the roof wall and thought for a moment. "You learn quickly, Miss James. He is certainly determined to find *something,* and you may well be correct. I am not my brother. His path wasn't for me. Oh yes, we grew up together in the camps—inseparable. There were so many of them, the WHO the UN, UNESCO, every letter under the sun. Jai was so young, but I remembered—I remembered enough that I was determined never to go back, to be successful enough that we didn't have to ever go back."

"But what about your parents?"

"Our parents? Jai has not told you?" he asked softly.

"He told me he had a family, father, mother and sisters ... "

"And that's true. We were taken out of the camps when he was four or five, adopted by a man Jai thinks of as his father, who had no sons of his own, just daughters. Jai was sent off to England, for what I believe they hoped would be a fresh start. I was older and wanted to stay here, to learn my foster father's business and earn my own money. When they, too, died, Jai's life took a different path, his way requiring him to fight, to struggle. He was courted by so many people; like brides they've come to him. No, not brides, more like thieves in the night with their lies and promises—Lashkar-e-Taiba,

Mujahideen, the Taliban, the Americans, the Haqqani, Jundallah, all of them wanted him because he had learned to fight, and he knows how to lead and they believe they can change him to their cause." He laughed. "He cannot be changed."

"I've noticed that."

The older man shook his head. "But it needs to stop. It doesn't go on forever. My brother is smart, brave and has been lucky so far. He needs someone, perhaps a woman, someone who is smarter, who *can* change him before his luck changes."

"I'm not sure that's me, Haafiz."

"Would you like it to be? There is a light in your eyes when you look at him. I see this!"

"Let me guess. Is my brother quoting Rumi at you?" Jai stood unnoticed in the shadows of the rooftop.

"Yes, and he's so charming, too. Weird how that's a trait you don't have in common!" I laughed.

He flung his arms around his brother affectionately. "And how cruel that I would be the only one to inherit the good looks."

"Get off me you goat!" Haafiz admonished. "I have no idea what it is you two are planning to do here, but I can only pray for you both, pray that you will both keep each other safe." He looked at his brother for a long time, before turning back to me.

"I regret I must leave you to the dubious care of this undeserving idiot, Miss James, but I wish you a good night, and wish you only luck and good fortune in your journey."

I thanked him. The moment he had gone I sunk my arms around Jai.

"These people haven't changed your mind about being here? You still want to go on?" he asked.

"I want to go on with you. I feel better here, Jai. This was good for me to be among your family."

It was dark on the rooftop; I could barely make out his features yet his eyes shone in the moonlight and his kiss, when it came, was a welcome surprise when it fell on my lips.

His hands lifted my hair as he kissed my neck.

"This is your brother's house," I whispered. "Is really nothing sacred to you Jai Khan?"

"Everything is sacred to me," he smiled back, as he slipped the kaftan from my shoulders. We made love under that big moon, on the roof of his brother's house, lost in each other, perhaps to forget that the next day we would meet with the fearsome tribal leader my country had labeled the region's public enemy number one, Siraj Sajjad.

The next day, Jai woke me early. The house was stirring and I knew we had a long way to go.

"Come on, sleepy; it's time," he said as we packed our things and prepared to leave.

In the courtyard, Haafiz and Nazneen were there to say their farewells. Now dressed in jeans, combat jacket and a *kaffiyeh* I had haggled over in the market at Cairo, I folded the kaftan Nazneen had given me and thanked her. She gestured me away.

"It is a gift, she says," Jai translated.

Haafiz embraced me, "God go with you."

"*Ma'a as-salaama*," I replied, already missing the warmth and generosity of their home.

We pulled out of the compound, a rugged looking Land Rover having replaced the smart town cars, and conspicuously without Jai's cadre of guards. Soon free of the suburbs we fell silent as we ascended the highlands to the foothills of the Hindu Kush, both lost in our own thoughts. The morning had dawned freezing cold and the difference in climate between the low steppes of Mazar-i Sharif and our current elevation was already noticeable, the brilliant blue skies of yesterday replaced with a somber grey. We drove still higher into ever steeper mountains, the roads petering out into nothing more than sheep trails, the colorless terrain making the driving slow going.

We traveled all day until, late in the afternoon, Jai pulled the Land Rover to the side of the trail. Rummaging from his bag, he gave me a pistol.

"They're likely to search me, but it's unlikely they would search you as a woman. It's a Glock—"

"... Glock 19. It has less recoil yet doesn't sacrifice accuracy, yes I know," I said matter of factly. I slid out the mag, reengaged it and armed the weapon smoothly, before disarming it again.

"Someone's been teaching you," he muttered, shaking his head with a smile.

"It seems like someone needed to." I replied.

He held me then, lightly, at arm's length as he seemed to like to do, his eyes locked on mine. "Look, I don't know how this is going to turn out..." he began.

"Reassuring as ever."

"It's just ... I just wanted to thank you," he said.

"Thank me for what?"

"For doing this, for being here with me...I wish I could offer you more, give you more in return Brea."

I looked at him for a long time by the side of that remote trail in the middle of nowhere, struggling with myself to try to unravel just exactly how I felt about him. I knew I didn't want to go anywhere, do anything, but stay with him like this, our eyes and maybe, for once, our minds locked together. I also knew we had a meeting to get to. A meeting that was important to him and that had now become crucial to us both.

Eventually I just said, "You know, sometimes you're a difficult man to love, Jai Khan," and I slid the gun into the waistband of my pants.

In the early evening we pulled into a small mountain village, seemingly deserted but for a line of what looked like military trucks and a gathering around a large tribal tent. In the distance a few herdsmen encamped with sheep nearby.

Jai was quiet, quieter than I had ever known him to be. In Cairo he had been calm, relaxed, even during the car chase through the city. Now he was quiet in a watchful, wary way. We parked the Land Rover and walked on foot to the encampment. As he approached, Khan stretched theatrically as if to ease the aches of the arduous drive, but I saw he was also taking in our surroundings and the shadowy figures who were undoubtedly taking up positions around us. When we arrived at the tent, a small wiry man dressed in all black robes and a long beard greeted us.

"As-salâmo alaykom," Khan said expansively, his hand over his heart and slightly bowing to the older man.

"*Wa Alykom As-salam,*" Siraj Sajjad replied unsmilingly, not acknowledging Khan's offer to embrace. He looked at Khan, then at me, then back to Khan with hooded, lively eyes, saying nothing. Sajjad bade us sit and, as is the custom, tea was prepared. I knew the meeting would be lengthy and even with Sajjad's apparent deference, as tradition demanded, no business would be discussed before it was offered. The conversation, such as I understood it, seemed to be in a mixture of Dari and Arabic.

Cups were provided and the tea, scalding and sweet, did at least provide welcome refreshment after our journey. At some point Jai asked, "*Âyâ šumâ englisi yâd dâren?*"

"I should speak English, for her?" Sajjad said.

"It is necessary."

"Necessary why?"

"She brings the funding arrangements. She represents the financiers of this very generous agreement."

"Your financiers being the Americans?"

Khan nodded. "Over our history we have traded with the British, the Russians and the Americans—they may not share our hearts, but we will gladly share their money."

Sajjad seemed unconvinced. "Then she is not your woman?" he pressed.

"She is not my woman." I winced a little at this, although technically I supposed it was true.

"And you trust her, this American woman?"

"I trust her with my own life."

"Your life matters very little to me, Jai Khan." He translated for the men nearest him and they all erupted into laughter at this.

Jai was unfazed and beamed back, "If the pleasantries are dispensed with, then perhaps it's time to see what we are buying."

Sajjad became businesslike again and abruptly rose and walked us out of the tent. We followed him to the first in the line of trucks and, ordering the back to be opened, he revealed its contents. Wooden or steel crates were piled on top of each other, each one stamped with U.S. Army, or with Russian or Chinese lettering. Pointing to one that was opened, even I could recognize from a dozen action movies the neat row of American military M16 semi-automatic assault rifles packed inside.

"Some Kalashnikovs and Russian junk but good rocket launchers and anti-tanks, mostly U.S. issued," the Sheik explained expansively. "Even our guest should approve," he smirked at me. "And here," he practically stroked a crate printed in what I recognized as Russian lettering, "see this—Bazalt RPG-7s. Never before used!"

I winced. It was abhorrent to me to think of what these weapons might be capable of.

"You could start a war with these treasures,' he went on, thoughtfully gazing at the deadly contents of the crate.

"Indeed, I intend to," Khan extolled. He was nothing if not convincing in a role as a radical terrorist leader, and it chilled me to hear him play the part with such easy conviction.

The other man chucked and gestured to an aide who gave me a folder piece of printed paper.

"So, now the money," he glowered at me.

Like so much else I was learning that they had got wrong, the CIA's assessment of Sajjad was completely inaccurate. In our short meeting he had revealed himself to be cautious and shrewd, but if they saw him as just a minor wrinkle in their plans to influence the future of the country, they were sorely underestimating him. I had no doubts he was capable of large-scale insurrection and the fact that only Jai had been able to make contact with him was proof of his illusive cunning.

I opened the laptop, checked the hotspot and after a moment received a passable signal. Idly I wondered if there was perhaps a CIA drone overhead watching all of this as I tapped in the information written on the note. It was a standard bank routing code and I recognized the address as being somewhere in Somalia.

"It is transferring?"

"It will take a minute, the signal really isn't strong out here," I said to Jai.

"Does she know what she is doing? Why the delay?" Sajjad asked more insistently.

Jai translated in Dari and the other man looked concerned. The signal faltered momentarily before commencing the transfer. The two financial institutions were connected to each other and the money was being transferred.

"It is done?" Sajjad repeated.

"It is done," I confirmed. The screen confirmed the transaction and the man looking over my shoulder nodded in agreement.

"Tell me, Jai Khan. The thing I find so curious is that you come to me with just this infidel girl, but where are your people? Where are all your loyal followers you hope to lead in your foolish jihad now, why don't I see them here?

If Khan was disarmed by the other man's sudden change in tone, he didn't show it. "There was no need to bring anyone else, our families, yours and mine, have been aligned for generations."

"And yet now you're allying yourself with the foreigners. I'm sure the Americans are already looking for you now; coming here was careless!" Sajjad was becoming visibly more excited and it worried me.

"*Naam,*" Khan dismissed in Arabic. "You are misinformed, my friend, no one knows we are here."

"It matters not; this arrangement is born of treachery. You mean to deceive us, Jai Khan, and because of that arrogance, we will be keeping our guns, and the girl will be a generous bonus as a hostage."

All around us I heard the sound of safeties being flicked off and arms raised.

"And tomorrow your infidel friends will find your wretched traitorous body picked over by the wild dogs," he smiled, and from beneath his robes he revealed a pistol, raising it immediately to Jai Khan's temple.

Things then happened in an instant. A red spot of light appeared momentarily on Sajjad's head and a split second later he reeled backwards, blood streaming from a sniper's single bullet. In the same moment, deafening gunfire erupted all around us, bullets thudding into the armament crates sending splinters flying, while other rounds clanged into the metal of the truck. Something that felt like a burning poker bit into my thigh as automatic fire skittered across the ground around us like deadly dust devils. Jai pushed to the ground and covered me with his body. The noise around us was deafening and brutal yet in a matter of seconds it was over.

In the eerie total quiet that followed I tried to comprehend what had just happened as Jai released me from his grasp. Sajjad was laying on the ground motionless in front of us, his hands still gripping the pistol. All around us, his bodyguards had been dropped where they stood. The man who had opened up the arms cache was slumped over the crates, his body riddled with bullet holes.

Out of the corner of my eye, behind Jai, I thought I saw something flash, a shadow of movement and something just clicked inside of me. Without thinking I reached behind me to the small of my back and found the shape of the gun in my hand. The adrenalin rushed around my body and without any kind of conscious thought, I squeezed the trigger just as I aimed past Jai's head. Behind him, Sajjad's bodyguard jumped as if electrocuted and then lay still.

Jai followed my gaze. "Brea?"

I winced, numbly.

"Brea?" he said again, the concern mounting in his voice. "Are you hurt?"

"I don't appear to be," I gasped, but I realized I was shaking. Everything had happened so fast; it was only just dawning on me that I had killed somebody. The awful realization of that fact seemed only numbed by the shock I was experiencing. Everything seemed to have happened so quickly yet, at the same time, the last few seconds seemed to have spanned a lifetime. Somehow, I moved my body, rolling over into a sitting position, Jai inched over to me, both of us still keeping low.

"That was quite a shot," he grinned. "For one crazy moment, I honestly thought you were aiming at me."

"I was. And I fucking missed," I managed to wheeze, not sure why I was finding it hard to breathe.

"Just stay there, take it easy," he said gently. "It seems like your sense of humor is still intact.

Behind the encampment, the herdsman whom I'd barely noticed earlier were approaching us holding automatic rifles, the apparent leader removed their head covering, the barrel of their H&K automatic still smoking. The thick, tousled hair and endless grin were unmistakably recognizable and Aliyah greeted us.

"Do I always need to be saving you?" she said, kissing Khan on both cheeks before moving to me, staring at the gun still in my hand then at the dead bodyguard, then back to me.

"Didn't I tell you you'd know what to do when the time came?" she said, grinning from ear to ear. Jai helped me to my feet, and Aliyah held me at arm's length to look at me, before completely enveloping me in an enthusiastic bear hug. Over her shoulder I could see the carnage all around us. It seemed all of Sajjad's men had been dropped within the first few moments of the gun fight. A sudden outbreak of new sporadic gunfire made me jump, before I realized Khan's men were probably finishing off the wounded fighters. The truck drivers, with their hands nervously above the heads clearly had no interest in the fight and were quickly surrendering to Khan's disciplined and better armed troops.

"Brea, you're hurt," Aliyah exclaimed, and when I looked down I saw dark red blood seeping from my pants. Weirdly, I hadn't noticed anything, just perhaps a feeling of hotness like shock from the gunfire, but as I tried to put my weight on my leg, I felt a pain like a red-hot poker jabbed into my thigh. Together they ushered me into Sajjad's tent and Aliyah unceremoniously pulled down my pants. Jai modestly looked away, but Aliyah clucked, "You two!"

"Now is not the time or place for you to be getting in my pants," I quipped through the pain, but to my alarm I could see now see the blood oozing from an open wound in my thigh. Aliyah calmly

159

staunched the bleeding while Jai prepared a makeshift tourniquet from his scarf.

"I think it's just a splinter or something. I'm fine," I said.

I saw the look from Jai to Aliyah and wondered what it meant. "Not a splinter, Brea, you took a bullet there," his voice sounded more concerned than I would have liked.

"It doesn't even hurt that much."

"It's the adrenaline," Aliyah said. "Give it time," and she went to fetch some supplies.

"Do I even want to know where the money is?" Jai asked quietly as he worked on my leg.

"Not where he wanted it," I nodded to outside the tent where the inert pile of rags that was Sajjad and his bodyguards lay.

Aliyah came back with some kind of antiseptic that burned enough to make me howl, and some antibiotics which she tipped down my throat with water from a flask. "That should do for now," Jai said covering my wound, "but we'll need to treat that; however, for now, we need to be moving." They both helped me to my feet and walked me unsteadily outside.

Now that the threat on the ground seemed diminished, I glanced nervously at the skies.

"Worried?" Jai asked.

"Aren't you? Drones, I mean?" I said nervously.

"I'm hoping we have thought of that eventuality," he said. "The CIA were provided some excellent intelligence that this transaction is in fact taking place a hundred miles way, when another of Siraj Sajjad's convoys of armaments is coming in from Pakistan."

Khan's men surrounded us and after a quick conversation, all cheered both their leader, and, apparently, me, as the savior of his life. Guns were fired randomly into the air along with some spirited roaring and chanting. Jai raised his hands and addressed them quickly and quietly in Pashto. To me he simply said. "Time to go." His men had commandeered the vehicles and, leaving the dead where they lay, we piled into the trucks and the convoy set off higher into the mountains. Whether it was the drugs or the adrenaline still coursing through my body, I don't remember feeling much pain as we left that abysmal little village. I was only glad to be away from there, and as we pulled out I shuddered as I saw the sky darken with crows circling expectantly.

We drove through the night, me dozing fitfully as Jai drove. As he had done piloting the jet, I marveled at his ability to keep awake, seemingly not needing sleep and occasionally checking in with other members of the convey on a cellphone, his gentle, hushed Pashto lulling me to sleep. At some point in the journey I woke, the pain in my leg nagging me awake.

"You knew about Sajjad?" I asked Jai as I peered into the darkness of the empty road ahead.

"Didn't know, no, but suspected. These people have been fighting for centuries—sometimes alongside each other as brothers, sometimes against as avowed enemies. You're in the insurance business, Brea, I'm sure you appreciate the need for a good back-up plan."

I did. Which was why I had built a mirror transaction site back in Cairo identical to the actual transfer software. All I had needed to do was type in the details Sajjad's man had given me and it would perfectly mimic the actions of an actual financial transfer. In other circumstances, the recipient would have no doubt confirmed the arrival of the monies with the receiving bank, but I was taking the chance—and it was a big chance—that Sajjad was either too greedy or too unclear on international finance and banking protocols to insist on that precaution.

In the early dawn of the next day we arrived at a small mountainside stop, where a small band of well-armed men mounted on sturdy Qataghani horses blocked the road and were waiting. Khan sensed my alarm and squeezed me hand.

"It's okay, we're just changing transportation," he said.

Dressed in warm traditional clothes with rolled woolen *pakuls*, these men were a sharp contrast to the sleekly dressed entourage that had met us at the airport. These were clearly fighters, men well used to hardship and life in the mountains, and I found myself again wondering at the breadth of Jai Khan's following. He greeted them warmly and I watched the men embrace and discuss what I assumed would be the next part of our journey, just as the first fine droplets of rain began to spatter on the windscreen.

I started as the door swung open and Aliyah climbed into the Land Rover from one of the trucks further back on the convoy.

"You okay?"

"Fine. Leg hurts, but I'm good. I thought being shot in the leg would hurt more."

"Don't worry, it will." She seemed distracted and absently turned on the windscreen wipers to watch the men. The rain was falling heavier now, hammering on the Land Rover roof, pooling in puddles in the road.

"What's the matter," I asked, "Are we in trouble?"

"We're always in trouble," she smiled ruefully. "Welcome to the life of a bandit."

"But Jai has the weapons, isn't everything going to plan—better than planned with Sajjad dead?"

"Maybe, but there's a price for everything. Now there are a lot more people looking for us and even in a country this big there are fewer places to hide."

"You mean drones?" I asked.

"Sure, drones, American patrols, government patrols, rival tribes. It's a list."

"But we're the good guys, Jai now has the protection of the American government—that has to count for something, even here," I insisted.

She looked at me warily. She seemed changed; that sunny optimism and humor that had sustained me at *Suaka Awan* seemed to now belong to someone else, a different woman. The brightly colored sarongs had been replaced with a flak jacket and boots. Her beautifully thick hair now tousled and muddy, the lethal Hecker & Koch maliciously slung across her lap and, when she looked at me, it was with the eyes of an older woman, their sparkle dulled with death and exhaustion.

"Try telling that to a drone pilot in Omaha who's seeing nothing but a long line of trucks carrying arms." She fell silent for a moment. "You know, Brea, when I left you that night at the embassy, I didn't think I would ever see you again." She seemed to stop herself, as if recalling something that was painful to her. "This is so fucked up," she exhaled quietly. "Jai really shouldn't have brought you here."

"He didn't. I came myself, and besides I think it will work," I ventured.

"Just listen to you. Now you're the one reassuring me," she smiled faintly. We watched in silence for a while as the men shouted instructions in the rain, the trucks continuing on their way, their cargo to be safety stashed until somewhere, at some time, destiny would need them. I felt her hand slide into mine.

"There's something I want to tell you," she said eventually in that same quiet voice, her eyes now restlessly scouring the mountains.

"Okay?"

"About what I said that night at the embassy. About how easy it would be if I'd had to kill you?"

I nodded. "How could I forget? That was sweet. Reassuring."

"That first time, Brea? The first time I fucked you was just business. Jai asked me to look after this uppity American bitch—that you were hysterical and I needed you to just calm down because, after all, we couldn't have you escaping into the jungle or waste time trying to find you. But I was wrong about that. I was wrong about you. I've had people I cared about before and when I left you at the embassy, I thought at least you'd be okay – you'd be safe. But seeing you here, in this place, with a bullet in your body, it's just a mess. I didn't intend this—any of this—for you."

"I'm fine ... " I started to say. I was shocked to see tears well in her eyes.

"Brea, you were hit with a high velocity round, most of it is still in you. Your femur is fractured, you've lost a lot of blood and out here we don't even have the ability to adequately clean the wound. Do you remember what you said to me on the boat when we were traveling back to Dhaka? You were right, this isn't your world, Brea. You're more than this; *you* mean something more to me than this." I felt her hand squeeze mine.

"I ..."

"Look, I really don't do this shit," she said, suddenly defensive. "I just don't need it, so you don't have to say anything, Brea. You just have to get out of here. You just have to live. Live your life, not ours...not *this*." The door of the Land Rover suddenly opened and she quickly withdrew her hand.

"We're going to need to get moving," Jai said, pausing for a moment as if sensing a change in the atmosphere in the Land Rover. Aliyah hurriedly brushed her face with her sleeve.

"Okay, we're ready," she said brightly. Jai gave me a questioning look as he took my arm over his shoulder and supporting me, we walked together to the band of horsemen.

"Do I want to know what you two were talking about?" he asked.

"Nothing. Girl talk," I yelped as I moved my leg into a more comfortable position, waving Jai's concern away. "Don't fuss," I said, wary of his men watching us, "I'm fine."

"Do you know how to ride, Brea?"

"I thought you already knew the answer to that, Jai," I wearily forced a grin and with his help, I swung myself up onto the saddle, grateful the horse wasn't taller as I felt the pain searing up my leg.

"We're going where it will be harder to find us," he explained reassuringly as an aide brought his own horse up. Swiftly mounting up, Jai trotted to the head of the small Uzbek raiding party and we headed immediately into the mountains, the rain quickly soaking us and swallowing us in the gloom.

As we climbed the temperature dropped alarmingly, and we had only just started. The small band rode day and night for three whole days, the scrubby mountain grassland turning to snow and ice. Rest stops were infrequent, and we constantly searched the skies as if it would be somehow possible to see any invisible assailant cruising watchfully above us. More worrying still, the pain in my thigh was now becoming worse. Jai was frequently dosing me with something I really hoped wasn't heroin, the plentiful drug of choice in these parts, which helped deaden the pain but also made me sleepy and even delirious. On the second day it became so cold, and I was so unsteady on my horse, that Aliyah beckoned to me.

"Here *Bibi*," she soothed, "come up and ride with me." I slid in front of her and she opened her quilted jacket, her body warming me, her hands folded over my breasts. I felt warmed, taken care of, loved almost. I dozed, night becoming day, the wind and coldness constantly nagging at me and the continual movement of the horse reminding me of the bullet buried in my leg.

We slept on our horses or at brief rests to enable them to rest. Jai forbad fires so we ate cold rice or bread. The days blurred into one long, tortuous ride. But at one point on the journey, I woke in the middle of the night. I felt lucid, better, and I stepped out of my blanket. It was cold in the moonlight and everyone was asleep, but on the ridge I could make out the outline of Jai Khan.

"You startled me," he said, opening his arms. "You're feeling better?"

"Much. It's weird but I feel the fever's gone," I replied drowsily and huddled against him.

"That's good, but that wound will still need to be treated," he sounded concerned.

We looked out across the desolate, cold plain. "I've been thinking, do you see there is some way … I don't know, some way we can be together?" I asked. Out here, the moon that had seemed so welcoming as we made love under it just a few days before, seemed cold and scornful.

"That's an interesting thought, seeing as I was just responsible for getting you shot."

"I think I got myself shot, but I'm serious, serious, Jai in a way that's fucking confusing to me."

"It will be hard, Brea … "

"I meant what I said in New York, Jai. I don't know when, or how, or even why, but I just know I'm so in love with you."

"You know that would mess up my plans for an arranged marriage to a political rival?"

"I get that," I laughed, "but you'll still need a skilled negotiator."

"In my tribal conferences or my bed?

"Both," I said and leaned against his chest

"I might have known you'd present a persuasive case," he smiled.

I wanted to hear more but he fell silent for a moment. "I'll die here, Brea," he whispered eventually. "Not in a car accident on Fifth Avenue, not of a heart attack, or in a modern, clean hospital surrounded by machines. I'll die here, out here. And you know, it doesn't bother me. Not anymore. It doesn't bother me because I have nothing much else to live for but this. I don't know what curious twist of fate brought us together, but I do know that if I let myself, it would be easy enough to forget it, forget all of this because I would have found something else to believe in, something stronger, something better. Because I would have found you."

"And you'd blame me for it."

"And I'd blame myself for it. Is that something you could understand?"

As rejection goes, that was probably one of the better ones.

"Why is this country so important to you, Jai? I persisted. "So desolate, so cold. The people are either so frightened or cruel?"

"That's what you see, and I can understand that you see that. But when I look out here I see people who can read and write, people who are uplifted by their religion, not afraid of it. I see technology and leaders like my brother in regimes that care, that have no time to be corrupt because they can see change happen. You see desolate valleys and plains; I see the Al Hambra Palace, cities rising like Samarkand, like Islamabad, full of culture, full of tolerance and understanding. Full of children who won't grow up afraid."

To hear him explain it was reassuring and, I realized as I nestled deeper into his chest and felt his arms around me, that I was happy, content that things were only as they were.

"Am I dying, Jai?" I whispered.

"Listen to me. I've lost so much in my life, Brea. I'm not going to lose you."

The image faded and I woke alone and colder than I'd ever felt before. I could only feel pain pooling around my body although I could barely feel my left leg at all. Aliyah was offering me water, holding my body upright.

"There, there, *Bibi*," she cooed, "you'll soon be home."

At that moment, in between illusion and the reality of the barren, cold windswept mountain, it didn't register quite what home might be. A Jai stronghold with fountains and a library? A cave encampment hidden in the desolate mountains? I dimly realized that our camp was already struck and the horse party was already mounted waiting for me. Aliyah flung my arm over her shoulder but when she helped me to my feet a groan escaped my throat so loudly everyone heard.

Aliyah shouted across to Jai something I couldn't understand. He looked at her and then at me in that way I had come to understand meant he was weighing something. There was something like sadness or regret on his face before he finally nodded silently to her.

"*Sheee* baby, not far now," she whispered to me and mounted me on the horse like a sack of potatoes, while she slid effortlessly behind me. I couldn't even feel the warmth of her body against me and I began wondering if I might perhaps already be dead, and that this all might be a horrible and endless nightmare.

If I had any memory of the night before, I dismissed it as a dream, and that day we climbed even higher, now high above the tree line, the ground hard and scattered with snow. Our party moved slowly, sometimes floundering in a deeper snow drift, sometimes dismounting and carefully guiding the horses across icy passes and sheer mountain drops. I was dimly aware of Jai ahead of us, spending much of that morning talking on his satellite phone. By mid-day the mountains temporarily opened up to a wide plateau and a high, flat meadow, a weak sun barely permeating the overcast sky. There were a few signs of life here. In the meadow someone had pitched a small tent next to a smoldering campfire, and incongruously at the edge of the meadow, an old DC9 propeller aircraft of a type you only see in old movies, and that I didn't know actually still flew, was partially hidden under the shadow of the mountains. At the head of our convoy, Jai signaled a stop and Aliyah slid off our horse and then carefully helped me down.

"Are we stopping?" I asked, groggily

"It's where *you* stop, Brea. You need to go home."

"You seem to say that to me a lot."

"Because you keep coming back to me!" She attempted a nervous laugh.

I was tired and sore, my mouth felt full of something like bile and I was grateful to dismount. As I looked around, I was aware for the first time of the intense activity around us. Horses were being watered, the camp was being packed up and fires doused. Jai had wheeled his horse around and reached us stragglers at the back of the convoy. Sliding off, he held me close, the anxiety obvious in his voice.

"How are you?"

"Fine, I'm good, really," I murmured, trying to stay on my feet.

"Brea, you must listen to me because we need to leave you now. We are still in great danger and need you to get out of here and to be safe."

"I ... I don't understand, Jai. I can't come with you to save the world?" I said, aware I was now noticeably slurring my words.

"It's not your fight, Brea, it never was, and now it's a dangerous one," he said, the concern written in his eyes. "It's time to get you home."

"And I'm to get home in that?" I jabbed my thumb at the antique plane, weakly attempting humor.

"I thought the Gulfstream might attract attention," he smiled, "and that's probably something best for all of us to avoid right now."

If I hadn't been so heavily under the influence of the drugs, I would have said something, done something—anything to prevent leaving Jai. Although even now I'm not sure what that might have been. That I would become his gangster moll? Scheherazade to his Shahryar? That I would spend the rest of my probably very short life in violence and hiding?

I heard him speaking in a blur.

"You will fly to Jordan tonight, and to a clinic I know where you can receive the treatment you really need for your wound. From there, I have contacts, people I trust, in Germany and then I've made arrangements for you to cross back into the States from Canada. After that, it is up to you; there will be nothing linking you to me, no trace of you even leaving the U.S." I was numbed, barely listening.

"I don't suppose for one minute I could convince you to come with me?" I ventured softly. "I'm beginning to realize I seem to have some influence with the world's law enforcement agencies."

He smiled, "I would love nothing more, but you need to get well, and I have work to do," he gestured at the line of riders, the horses snorting and pawing impatiently.

"Then take this." I fumbled in my bag and dug out the cloth bag containing the Goddess. "You'll need her." I shoved the small, cloth-bound bundle into his hands.

"No!" he shook his head. "I can't. After everything you've been through? What about your commission? All of it— it would have all been for nothing for you."

I looked at him, this towering man, now seemingly so small against the spectacularly desolate backdrop of the mountains.

"Not quite nothing," I mumbled, aware that my eyes were filling with tears. "It belongs to you; it belongs to your people. We both know now that my clients weren't even a legit auction house, I would never have been paid anyway. And in my country it will sit in some dusty case in a wealthy museum and no one will even know what she is. Here, with you, at least there's a chance she can stand for something."

"But wasn't this—all of this, wasn't it about the Goddess all along?"

"It was never about the Goddess, Jai. I understand that now. The Goddess was nothing more than an excuse, a front for everything they wanted to hide. The CIA couldn't care less now, and I can say it was lost, destroyed, which would be highly likely. My country will have gained more than they paid for if you succeed, Jai. That will be enough."

"I will succeed, Brea, and you've played a big part in making sure we can bring peace to this country. He pressed the bundle back into my hands. "But you should be the one to take care of her, Brea. I know you will do the right thing by the Goddess."

"Well then," I said holding out my hand, and immediately aware of the tears that were betraying me. "Go build your country, then. It's been a pleasure doing business with you, Mr. Khan."

"As with you, Miss James." Taking my hand, he pulled me to him, his mouth hungrily on my lips.

I don't remember us breaking our embrace. I don't remember feeling the loss of his arms around me. I remember him whispering something beautiful sounding in Arabic and receiving a warm lingering embrace from Aliyah. After that, I think I drifted in and out of consciousness. I felt strong hands holding me up and was dimly aware of watching Jai, Aliyah and that small band of his most trusted followers heading up further into the mountains. At that moment I remember thinking how impossibly handsome he looked on a horse, in a tux, flying a plane, doing everything, doing anything. I watched their diminishing trail of dusty snow fade into the horizon as, behind me, I heard the aircraft engines splutter into life with a roar that filled the meadow, and the pilot in halting English telling me it was time to go. He helped me, with some difficulty, onto the plane and into a seat, firmly strapping me in. The interior of the airplane was cold and noisy and as we rattled down the short grassy runway I wondered if we would even make it. At seemingly the last minute, and at the very edge of the meadow, the ancient aircraft lifted off, just above the precipice. I frantically looked out of the window as we banked alarmingly over the mountain to see if I could see the horse party but, as we turned to head west, all I could see through the blur of my own tears was the endless desolation and emptiness of the mountains.

POSTSCRIPT

I. | AMMAN, JORDAN

Off of the bustling souk in the old quarter, and down from Amman's old Roman amphitheater, I entered an internet café on Al-Qadeseyah Street and ordered a coffee. Choosing an old, battered IBM near the window I quickly disengaged from the café's internet and connected the hotspot on the burner phone. Dialing up a number, there was a momentary silence before I heard the distant ringing tone and shortly after a familiar voice came through my headphones.

"Miss James, you never cease to surprise us."

"One of these days you're really going to have to explain who the 'us' is, but for now there is some unfinished business we have to discuss, and we don't have much time."

"Well then, I'm all ears."

"I'd like to propose a deal."

"And here was I foolishly laboring under the belief that you were making all your own arrangements these days?"

"Come now, Jonathan, you know I've always been your girl. Didn't you get me naked in the back of your car?"

I could almost hear an embarrassed smile through the long-distance delay.

"Yes, quite, but you have to admit Cairo was a bit of a mess now, wasn't it? The authorities there are still scratching their heads trying to understand exactly what happened."

"Are they now?"

"Indeed. As it happened my people were fortunate enough to be able to lift some fascinating prints from the steering wheel of an otherwise burnt-out vehicle we found abandoned in the desert."

"That *is* fascinating, Jonathan."

"The file is on my desk here, but I confess I'm running a bit behind on my paperwork and I'm not totally sure I'll find it. Unless, of course, I need to."

"I'm hoping once we're done here you won't find that necessary."

"Yes quite, but I think even you'll agree that recent events have not quite followed the plan we had carefully—and you'll forgive me if I repeat the word—but *carefully* discussed."

"On the contrary, I believe it's exactly the plan we discussed," I replied. "After all, Siraj Sajjad is dead, as you had clearly wanted, and the CIA now has someone who has a decent shot of seizing power, and with whom they can actually deal with for a change. If I say so myself it was a nice bit of negotiating all around, not to mention selflessly involving some considerable risk on my behalf."

There was a pregnant pause on the other end suggesting that some of what I'd just told him was news to Byrne.

"I forget, restitution is your game, Miss James, and I'm reminded that risk is also something you believe you understand."

"I believe I do. But there is one small a condition."

There was an audible sigh at the other end of the line, "Miss James?"

"No more interfering with our lives: Immunity, for both myself and for Khan."

"That's not mine to give, Brea, I think you know I'm a humble servant …"

"I don't care who you work for, but I think we both know that's a crock. You are clearly more than some Interpol beat cop, and since we both know you're tracing this signal, your window for agreeing to this very satisfactory deal is rapidly expiring. You'll also notice, by the way, there's some 50 million dollars missing from the CIA household budget."

Byrne's cool demeanor took on a little edge. "That's theft, Miss James, and it would be a mistake."

"From where I come from it's called insurance, and the mistake is entirely yours to make. For now, it's sitting safely in an unnumbered offshore account, but I want the U.S. taxpayer to have her money back, so immunity, and the amount will be immediately returned." I let that sit with him for a while and took a sip from the thick black Jordanian coffee, savoring the peppery, citrusy blending of lemon and cardamom. Outside in the sun-dappled street I watched tourists haggle with a market stall vendor in an ancient dance. It seemed such a contrast to the technology our voices were traveling through, thousands of miles through relays and satellites to the no doubt darkened room from where Jonathan was speaking, around him operatives frantically tapping into computers to trace the call.

Eventually he broke the silence. "Very well, if everything you say is true, then I think we can come to an agreement. But if your

Khan turns out to be the next Bin Laden, I hardly need to mention that the consequences will be very bleak—and not just for the both of us."

"I think we both know that's not going to be the case. And as a bonus I hope to selflessly continue to initiate delicate diplomatic negotiations with Khan myself, whenever possible and at no cost to the government," I said, and then, in what I hoped was a more serious tone, "you know, Jonathan, he's going to be a leader we'll want to work with."

"You certainly present a very persuasive case, Miss James."

"I certainly hope to."

"And I'm compelled to remark that for someone who seems to have a singular inability to follow simple instructions, I have to admit you've demonstrated something of a flair for this line of work."

"Me? I'm just a humble insurance adjuster, Mr. Byrne."

"In that case, may I assume this call never took place, Miss James?"

"It never did."

I cut the connection, gathered my things and, betraying a smile impossible to conceal, I walked out of the café, disappearing into the bright sunshine and crowded bustle of the street.

II. | KABUL, AFGHANISTAN

Yahira El-Masri had paid little attention to the package that had arrived in his office earlier that day. The Director of the Kabul National Museum had been busy with tedious administrative affairs, but just before leaving his office for the *adhaan* call to prayer, the compact orange and white DHL courier box again caught his eye. Carelessly breaking the seal, El-Masri noted the sender's address; it was not one he was familiar with; it appeared to be from some corporate address in Jordan. Whatever it was, the contents were well protected with layers of polystyrene foam and bubble wrap, and he was beginning to tire of the effort. Yet as he pulled aside the last layers of packing, he found it difficult to believe his eyes.

"Taeal 'iilaa huna!" he yelled out excitedly to his clerk. The boy rushed into the office at the commotion and immediately skidded to a halt when he recognized the diminutive figurine the Director was cradling in his hands. The Sarianidi Goddess was finally home.

ACKNOWLEGEMENTS

Predictably, Brea only came into the world with the love and support from too long a cast of characters than can be accurately listed here. I don't possess enough gratitude to thank Caryn for, as always, being my patient first proof reader and for the financial midwifery to help birth this adventure. I have to thank the lovely and irrepressible Linzi Drew for her early encouragement and for sharing some of her charmed ability to describe strong, resourceful women. My thanks also to Larry Spinrad, who's been here before, and whose advice on how to 'stop thinking about it and just start writing' was my mantra, and, of course, to the always kick-ass Cindy Zimmer, for long ago patiently explaining the thing about the commas, and for so much more. After long days sitting at my desk in Brea's world, the generous and gifted Dr. Nadrine Omar miraculously healed my aching body, although fixing my terrible and limited Arabic proved far more challenging. Stockholm Syndrome was polished, edited, bound and ushered into being by Ramona Pina and my amazing publishing team at Book Baby and is offered in memoriam to my friend Paul who, like Brea, was an exceptionally courageous traveler through life and who I'd like to think would have also found wonders at the Souk in Cairo.